whispers

and the

ROARS

k webster

dedication

To my handsome voice of reason,
Your whispers keep me sane.
Your roars keep me safe.
I love you.

From *USA Today* bestselling author K Webster comes a gripping and emotional psychological romance standalone!

I'm a recluse.
Sad, quiet, afraid.
Sequestered in my home away from the world.
It's better this way.

I wasn't always alone.
I had him—my boyfriend, my best friend, my everything.
Yeo Anderson.
But I sent him away.

I was a fungus. Growing and festering. Turning his brilliant parts black with the disease otherwise known as me.

My sweet boy was sick in love. I couldn't bear to think about what he was giving up. For me. I'd poisoned him, but it wasn't too late. I could fix it. So, I did.

But he's back.
The boy blossomed into a man who wants to fight me for me.

The past that rules me is dark and chaotic and violent.
It always wins.

Love isn't supposed to be a war.
Yeo thinks our hearts, though, will win this time.

Warning:

Whispers and the Roars is a dark romance. Strong sexual themes and violence, which could trigger emotional distress, are found in this story. The abuse written in this story is graphic and not glossed over, which could be upsetting to some. This story is NOT for everyone. Proceed with caution.

"You are terrifying and strange and beautiful, something not everyone knows how to love."

Warsan Shire

A note to the reader before beginning...

This book took the longest for me to write out of any of my books. It was mentally overwhelming at times and required a lot of research on my part. I've exhausted a lot of energy into making this story as authentic as possible.

This isn't a typical romance.

There is nothing typical about this story.

I'm asking you to go into this book with an open mind. I want you to turn off what you know and soak in what I am slowly pouring into you. I'm asking for you to read this story without preconceived notions or ideas.

This story, while at times can be difficult to comprehend, is a beautiful one if you see it all the way through.

Unconditional love, understanding, and ultimate dedication are the themes of this novel.

Thank you for reading. Make sure you find the link in my note after the story to guide you to the discussion room where you may speak freely about the story without fear of spoiling it for anyone.

Thanks,
K Webster

prologue

Kady
The Past

When my eyes are closed, the monster can't see me.
When I sing a song in my head, the monster can't hear me.

When I pretend my bedroom is a playground where I play hide-and-seek, the monster can't find me.

The darkness should frighten me.

I should worry I'll find *more* monsters…monsters scarier than *him*.

But I'm not afraid.

It's safe here.

When I'm inside of my head…

He. Can't. Ever. Touch. Me.

chapter one

Kady
The Present

The sick stench of stale cigarettes and cheap beer lingers in the air. I can always tell when he's been by looking for me. Clues are scattered about the house—as if he leaves them on purpose. To taunt and fuck with me. A half-empty pack of cigs. A tipped, dripping can of Budweiser crushed and discarded on the kitchen table. His name carved into the wood beside the can. Sharp. Edgy. Imperfect. *Norman.*

Beads of sweat form on my upper lip, and I rush to the front door in an effort to breathe without breathing *him* in. The moment I swing it open, a cool late spring breeze whips inside around me, lifting my damp hair off my sticky neck.

I can't believe I managed to stay away while he was here. I'm always afraid he'll find me. That he'll drag me up to my bedroom, pull my sweaty clothes from my thin frame, and terrorize me like he's been doing since I was old enough to utter the word "daddy."

A squawk from the horn of a bike causes me to jolt from my daze, and I awkwardly wave at Christopher, a twelve-year-old kid from up the street. He waves back, but I notice the way his legs work harder to propel his bike past my house. Away…from me. Christopher, like most of my neighbors, dislikes me. Some may even fear me, which is ridiculous. I'm just a broken twenty-nine-year-old. Not a monster.

A recluse. I'll give them that.

At one point in time, I wasn't. At one time, someone could pull me from my sad world, show me that shards of light could shine through, and let me feel true love. Life, at one time, was as perfect as life could be for me. At one time, I'd had hope.

But then he left me too.

Not that I can blame him. I would've left me too if I were him. It still hurt, though. No, it fucking gutted me to my core. Actually, there isn't even a way to describe what I felt the moment he was gone.

A part of me died.

Burned and charred, then simply blown away ash by ash the next time a breeze rolled on by.

My belly growls and I wonder if Aunt Suzy or Agatha have been by the grocery store yet. Money is tight these days, but Aunt Suzy is a hard-core coupon cutting queen. She somehow manages to feed this wild family on a tiny budget provided by the state and my meager earnings. If things get too rough, Officer Joe always stops by with burgers or a loaf of bread and some peanut butter. He was the responding officer that night the shit hit the fan. And twenty years later, he still checks up on his favorite Kady Bug.

I may be a lonely woman, but I have some amazing people who look after me.

Too bad the one I miss the most ran off to Yale University. Left his girlfriend to pursue a career. Stole my heart right from my chest.

You would have held him down, Kady. He was meant to soar.

Tears well in my eyes, but I blink them away. It's easy to forget I'm the one who encouraged him to leave. To follow his dreams—dreams that didn't involve me. I was a fungus. Growing and festering. Turning his brilliant parts black with the disease otherwise known as me. When you're a woman who suffers from depression and PTSD, among other disorders, you learn that you're the problem. That you're the source of nightmares. That you're a black plague who only sickens the well around you.

And my poor, sweet boy was becoming sickened. He was sick in love. His father hated me for it and was disappointed in his son. I couldn't bear to see the one I love—the one who always smiled brilliantly just for me—frown and ponder. To see his eyes cloud over and become distant as he thought about what he was giving up. For me.

I made the decision for him, so he wouldn't have to. He wouldn't even choose air or food or water over me. And that's exactly why he couldn't stay. I'd poisoned him, but it wasn't too late. I could fix it.

So I did.

My stomach grumbles again and I frantically look

around for Aunt Suzy. There's no way I can go to Walmart. The place is crawling with people and that makes my skin crawl too. I can't stand the way they all dissect me with their eyes. How the women in this town crowd around me and fuss over me, like a gaggle of obnoxious geese, as if it's their duty because they knew my grandma. The way they all try to figure out *why* I'm a monster. I hate the way they look for him—*Norman*—when they see me. A man who would do heinous things to his own flesh and blood. They turn my carefully constructed world upside down. Madness and chaos take over until I'm begging for my bed and peace and the one who still holds my bleeding heart in his hands.

I need quiet.

I need order.

A reprieve from the roars.

My world offers me the briefest glimpse of happiness when I'm able to silence the deafening chaos in my little town.

I can survive when it's only the whispers.

Deciding Walmart is a very bad idea, I close the front door and dispose of Norman's demonic debris. Agatha will chide me for cleaning up after him, but I do it anyway. It's empowering to rid my home of his remnants. Once the air smells of Febreeze—we've got forty-seven cans thanks to one of Aunt Suzy's coupon hoarding moments—I make my way over to the piano in the living room. The piano is my getaway from the pain. I find solace in the music—the cadence that slows my thrumming heart to a beat that doesn't have it threatening to jump from my chest and run down the street toward the tan house on the corner.

I lift a window to let some cool air in and to filter out the stench of the cigarette smoke that still taints the air around me. The air conditioner is broken again but money is tight. Bones left a note for me yesterday saying he'd get it fixed, but I'm still here sweating my ass off. He's not usually one to follow through. Unlike him, I can't walk around with no shirt on twenty-four-seven. I'll have to see if Agatha knows someone who could repair it inexpensively.

My heart is achy today. I know I'll need to perk up before my piano lessons later this afternoon with Kyra. She's nine and has been working hard to master all of the songs in her beginner's book. The girl is an avid learner. Quite determined for her age. When my mood is dark, she senses it and *Mary Had a Little Lamb* becomes intense and eerie. So I try to shower her with my smiles and radiate happiness.

Until then, though…

I slide onto the worn, wooden bench seat, my bare thighs under my cutoff shorts sticking to the surface. Tugging a hairband from my wrist, I brush my hair into a ponytail with my long fingers. It's damp underneath and it feels amazing to get my heavy hair off my neck. I twist it into a messy bun then lay my fingertips on the aged ivory keys. Long ago, Grandma taught me how to play. It ended up becoming my therapy—my only escape. Now, it's my supplemental income. A few brave parents pay me for lessons for their children, but only after they realized that I'm not the evil person the town claims I am.

Silencing my thoughts, my fingers begin fluttering over the keys. Haunting sounds from *The Secret Letter* fill my home. I play the piece not from memory, but from the soul.

The music is an extension of my pain and sadness. A direct view into the mind of a woman who has spent an entire lifetime attempting to forget injustices served against her.

Only I *can't* forget.

Not when Norman still comes around.

Not when Grandma's empty bedroom makes me cry.

Not when the love of my life exists in another town *without* me.

But when I'm playing the piano, albeit for a brief moment, I'm able to forget. I'm able to silence those roars. Turn them into whispers. Let the music flood my soul and drown the horrors of my past.

When I play, I'm content.

Even if only for a little while.

chapter two

Yeo

The tight ball of anxiety that always twists my heart is finally relaxing its hold. Twelve years is a long time to have that part of you in a vise grip. Kadence Marshall has been my entire world since I was ten years old. And now, every single choice. Every single decision. Every thought that enters my mind…involves her. It's always been that way and it always will be that way.

I love her.

Plain and simple.

You can't snuff out the blazing flames of love.

Soulmates don't simply drift apart.

Twelve years has done nothing to change the way I feel about her.

The time with us separated is over.

No more hiding.

No more avoidance.

No more denying our complicated relationship.

I'm going to make this right again.

She pushed you away, Yeo.

It was the push I needed, though. She *was* right. I couldn't help her with no education, no home, no money. Instead of hating her or obsessing over the whys of how she could push me away, I chose to run in the opposite direction toward something that would eventually bring us back together. Kady is the type of woman who deserves a lifetime commitment.

Sometimes there isn't a quick fix or an easy solution.

Often, these things take time.

When you're dedicated to someone completely, you take that time and you make it work for you.

She is one commitment I never thought twice about. I'd ignored my father's pleas to go to school for business management. Running his multinational technology company was something my brothers could do alongside him. Anderson Tech was doing just fine without me. The baby. The rebel. The brother from another mother.

I smile as I think about my mother. Gyeong Anderson is a force to be reckoned with. Over thirty years ago, she'd fallen in love with my father while he spent a few years in South Korea for business. She'd gotten pregnant with me very early on in their relationship. Problem was, Dad was already married. Already had two boys, Dean and Barclay. When he realized what a mess he'd made, he ended up divorcing Evelyn so he could marry my mother. Dad wanted all of his children in West Virginia. Together. One happy, screwed-up family.

Dad bounced back and forth between their stunning

brick home on the newer end of Morgantown and our sim-ple house at the end of Kady's street. He may have been legally married to my mom, but he was still a devout father to my brothers. To say it was an easy upbringing would be laughable. But I was loved and taken care of my entire life. I couldn't ask for much more.

Kady fits in somehow. I just know it. And soon, we're going to figure out how. I've spent a lot of time working toward this moment. It's going to work.

A shrill ringing jars me from my thoughts and I scram-ble for my cell phone, careful to keep my eyes on the road.

"Hello?"

"Dad tell you we're having dinner tonight at LeBlanc's Steakhouse?" Barc questions, launching into what he's called for without so much as a greeting.

He's the middle Anderson son, and the one who resem-bles Dad the most. Tall, dark brown wavy hair, broad shoul-ders, and a hard scruffy jaw. Dean looks a lot like Evelyn with lighter brown hair and softer features. Of course, I bear the least resemblance to our father due to my South Korean ethnicity. I'm tall like Dad and can bulk up when I need to, but my eyes are almond-shaped and brown like my mother's. My hair is stick straight and black.

"Who's we?"

"Patty, the twins, Mom and Dad, Dean and his new girlfriend, and of course Gyeong. The usual," he grunts out. I can tell he's at the office because I can hear him tap-ping away on his computer as he speaks. Barc never stops working. His marriage to Patty is on the rocks because of it, too. If it weren't for the twins being so heavily involved in softball and starting high school, I think she'd have left him already.

"Can I bring a date?"

The tapping stops and his breathing becomes ragged. He doesn't have to say anything. I can almost hear the questions bouncing around in his mind.

Is it her?

Kadence Marshall?

What will she fuck up now?

But he won't ask. He's not as bold as Dad and actually gives a rat's ass about his brother's feelings.

"Sure, man. Bring a date. Is he hot?" His trying to play off the tense moment brings a smile to my face.

Chuckling, I shake my head. "Fuck off. You know I'm into chicks, not dicks."

"That's not what the rumors say," he teases.

I tense momentarily at his words but then shake it off. The rumor mill in this town is huge and always running.

"Yeah, yeah. What time?"

"Reservations are at eight."

We hang up and I hit the accelerator on my BMW. I caught all kinds of shit back in Connecticut, where I completed my residency at Saint Francis hospital, for driving this yuppie car. It wasn't worth defending myself, though— my peers just don't understand my family. Dad gifted it to me once I completed my M.D. While my colleagues were drowning in student loan debt those four years after and taking the bus to work, I was rolling around in an eighty-six thousand dollar M6 convertible and living in my paid-for-by-daddy loft in downtown Hartford.

He'd wanted to buy Mom a gigantic house, like the one he and Evelyn lived in, but my mother insisted on the tan house she still lives in. Her house cost less than my damn car. She's about the only person he lets get away with telling him how it's going to be. I'll never understand their relationship.

Mom once told me she's a fire-breathing dragon and that Dad is flammable. I didn't ask much more on the subject.

I'm dying to call Kady. We've spoken a handful of times over the last twelve years. Sometimes Mom checks in on her for me. Mostly I've kept up with her by Facebook messaging Agatha about her. And on occasion when I try and call, I have to talk to *him*.

Bones.

Arrogant. Ballsy. Doesn't give a damn about rules or logic or reason.

And my best friend.

It's always him I end up speaking to when I call since she won't answer. If I can hold out until I get back to Morgantown, though, I can find a way to talk to her. It's been hell all these years with her avoiding my calls and hiding anytime I'm in town to visit. I know she's not seeing anyone, but she's still impossible to reach.

But now that I'm moving back, she can't hide any longer.

I'm coming for my girl once and for all.

Whether she likes it or not.

And Bones can fuck right off if he thinks he's going to keep her from me. As soon as that thought enters my mind, guilt threatens to suffocate me. It's not his fault. At least he answers. The only person keeping me away from Kady is Kady.

With a sigh, I speed dial her house. I always hope she'll answer. Just this once.

"Yo!"

I cringe at hearing his voice. "Where's Kady?"

"Nunya."

Gripping the steering wheel, I swallow down my irritation. "What?"

"Nunya business." He laughs and I want to throttle him.

"Come on, man. Just get her for me. I need to ask her something," I say, my voice tight in my attempt to control myself from getting angry with him. Losing my temper with Bones just gives him the upper hand. I know this from experience. And I won't let him win.

"We'll play Telephone. You tell me and then I'll tell her. Then," he says with a chuckle, "I'll tell you she said to fuck off." Despite the humor in his voice, I can read between the lines. He's still pissed over our last encounter. Once again, guilt surges through me.

The line goes dead and I pull the phone away from my ear. Dammit. When he's angry with me, he always plays these stupid games. Games I don't know how to play. Games I could care less to play. But games I nonetheless *have* to play.

"I'm done playing Telephone," I grumble aloud. "Because I'm about to play Knock, Knock…and that's a game where I *always* win."

I emerge from Mom's house with a bounce in my step and determination moving me forward. For lunch, she fattened this hardworking boy up with a heaping plate of samgyeopsal and a side of kimchi. I didn't realize how much I'd missed Mom's cooking until after my second plateful. If it were up to me, she'd be making my welcome home dinner rather than LeBlanc's. I can get steak anywhere, but good South Korean *home* cooking is hard to come by on the east coast.

The walk to Kady's is a short one. I remember riding my bike to her house hundreds of times back when life was simpler. Back when we were friends. Back when we were filled with beginnings of more. Back when I thought I'd die if I couldn't breathe her in every second of every day.

But life caught up to us.

Reality became something I had to deal with.

Luckily for us, I'm a problem solver. Our hurdle was just that. A hurdle. And now I'm ready to swoop her in my arms, apply a salve to her battered heart, and finally make her mine. Every broken piece of her. Mine.

As I near her house, the first thing I notice is the paint chipping away. The porch seems to be sagging on one side. The grass is overgrown. My heart aches in my chest. A sense of responsibility washes over me, and I want to beat the shit out of myself for letting this happen.

Not anymore.

Not ever again.

When I hear *Row Row Row Your Boat* being played on

the piano, I slow my steps. My intention had been to barge in there, find my girl, grovel at her feet, and fix this shit. But, if she's working, I can't do that. At least not yet.

I wait patiently on the bottom step until a young girl with a long black braid down the middle of her back eventually emerges. She bounds down the steps right past me, locates her bike laying on its side in the driveway, and then takes off. Without hesitating, I rise to my feet and stride up the stairs to the front door. After all this time, I should knock. But with Kady, it's best to catch her by surprise.

"Kady?" I call out as I push through the door. The first thing I notice is how damn hot it is and wonder why the air conditioner isn't on. It'll be unbearable by summer. The unit is either on the fritz or Suzy is trying one of her money saving techniques. Either way, I'm going to deal with it.

I'm met with silence. The piano has been abandoned. Kady's flip-flops have been left under the bench and a cold bottle of water sits on a coaster nearby. I open my mouth to call out to her again when I hear the creak of a floorboard. Lifting my gaze, a smile plays at my lips until I meet the bored gaze of fucking Bones.

His shoulder is leaned up against the wall and his shirt is gone as usual. It irritates me that he walks around half naked every time I see him. Especially since kids are in and out of this house for lessons all the time.

"Where's Kady?"

He shrugs and saunters over to the sofa, ignoring my question. I grit my teeth when he sits down and shoves his hand into his pocket only to pull out a wooden dugout used to hold his marijuana paraphernalia. He twists the top and slides out a pinch hitter in which he smokes it from. I watch with irritation as he uses his pinky to smash the weed into the end before locating his Zippo. With a flick of the metal lid, he brings the flame to the end of his pinch hitter and takes a deep hit.

Kady would be furious if she knew he was toking it up in her living room.

"You should quit that shit, man," I say with a growl and stride over to the armchair. Once I sit, I lean forward, place my elbows on my knees and meet his bloodshot eyes. "I want to see her. Where the hell is she?"

He takes another hit before answering me. "She doesn't want to see you. Obviously. Besides, you fucking broke her goddamned heart when you left. You think she ever wants to see you again?" His words sting and his eyes flicker with regret. I can read Bones just as easily as I can read Kady. We were The Terrible Three back in the day. Now, we're nothing.

I run my fingers through my now sweaty hair and I can feel it sticking up in every which direction. I'll need a shower before dinner tonight. Bones watches my action with a narrowed gaze and his eyes flash with anger. "We both know she pushed me away, Bones. She pushed and pushed and pushed. But guess what? I'm done being pushed. I know what I want. I want her. And I don't care if I have to drag her out of this hell hole and into my arms to do it."

He sneers. "Cue the fucking singing clowns. Let's all bow down to the great Dr. Anderson. He's finally decided he wants his girlfriend back."

I take a deep, calming breath. "She and I can fix what

we have. I just need to see her."

"She's seeing someone else," he taunts. "Someone better looking. Someone who fucks like a champ. Someone like me."

At this I laugh, but it's a bitter sound. "We both know you're not seeing her. Your communication skills leave something to be desired."

He stiffens at my words. "Fuuuuuuuuuck."

I lift an eyebrow. "What?"

"I told her I'd find someone to fix the damn air conditioner. Hell if I didn't forget," he grumbles. "I'd been on my way to see my buddy Davey to buy a half ounce. I was supposed to ask his neighbor if he'd come take a look. But damn if Davey's sister wasn't all up on my nuts with her tongue in my ear whispering all the shit she wanted to do to me. I fucking got distracted by her big tits and those pepperoni-sized nipples that taste like heaven."

Closing my eyes, I inhale a deep breath and clench my fists. When I finally reopen my eyes, he's watching me with interest.

"You got a thing for Davey's sister too? I'd share her with you, pretty boy. Bitch probably likes double penetration or some shit. I can tell that gets your dick hard, Yeo." He licks his lips suggestively. "Want a hit?"

He holds out his pinch hitter to me and I shake my head. "I want to take her to dinner tonight. Can you pass on the message?"

"Yep." His eyes flicker with dishonesty and I shake my head.

"Actually, I'll leave her a note instead."

I stand and stride from the room into the kitchen. Agatha keeps the kitchen immaculate. It always smells of bleach and oranges. Beside the phone on the countertop is a pink sticky note pad with a big A at the top. I rip off a page and then find a pink Sharpie.

Kady,

> *I know you're avoiding me, beautiful, but time's up. No more running. I promised I'd be back for you and you know I keep my promises to you...in this case, whether you like it or not. I have to attend a celebratory dinner with my family that I'd love for you to come to and then afterward it would just be us. We can talk and catch up. Kiss like we used to. I want to see your sweet smile and pretty eyes. I want to run my fingers through your soft hair. I want to hear about what's upsetting you and what makes you happy.*
>
> *I just want...you.*
>
> *I miss you and I love you. Always have, always will.*
>
> **Yeo**

Once I'm done, I leave the note on the counter and start out of the kitchen only to slam right into Bones. I'm taller and bulkier than him, so I end up knocking his bony ass to the floor.

"Fucking brute," he complains from on his ass on the squeaky clean linoleum.

Smirking at him, I reach down, holding my palm out to him. He waves me away and climbs to his feet without my help. I try not to inspect the new tattoos on his chest since I last saw him. It'll only irritate me more.

His gaze inspects my frame like he's sizing me up. "You stink." His lip curls up in disgust. "Fucking kimchi."

I laugh and ruffle his sweaty hair. "Says the asshole who smells like a dog. Tell Kady I'll call a repairman. I'm coming for her later whether you approve or not. And for the love of all that's holy, take a shower, man."

He flips me off, but I don't miss the smile on his face. As much as I hate to admit it, I missed this house and all the weird people in it. I missed Bones too.

I'm almost back to Mom's when a car engine rattles from behind me. As soon as my gaze meets that of Kady's aunt Suzy, I nearly leap in front of the car to stop it.

"Suzy!" I shout at her.

She stops the car and leans her head out of the window. A floral print scarf is wrapped around her head and she's wearing a godawful pair of ugly, oversized gold sunglasses. "Yeo, sweetheart!"

I trot after her and climb into the passenger seat. As soon as I'm inside, she yanks me to her in a fierce hug. When she pulls away, her smile is broad. God, it feels good to be back home.

"Would you look at you, boy? You done turned out to be one handsome fella! Are you seeing anyone? Because I tell you, I'm not too old to take a young lover. I tell you what, I know a few tricks—tricks only old ladies know— and I could really make you happy, sweetie."

When I laugh, she cackles. Only Suzy cackles loud enough to wake the dead. Most people cringe when she laughs, but I can't help laughing with her. "You know I only have eyes for one girl."

She pretends to pout as she puts the car into drive. "Fine, but I'm kidnapping you. We're going to Walmart. Kady left me a list a mile long of stuff we need. I tell you, if Bones doesn't stop eating us out of house and home, I don't know what we're going to do. That boy loves his Cheetos," she confides. "You know, they don't let you double up on coupons anymore. Did you know that? About three years ago, those nincompoops grew some brains and realized they were paying us to shop. It was a fun run while it lasted, huh? I still have enough toilet paper in our basement to keep our behinds wiped through the apocalypse if need be. Does Gyeong need any extra? We have loads extra. And you better believe we'll have the cleanest teeth during the end of days. The Two Dollar Store once paid me forty-seven dollars to take a hundred and sixteen tubes of toothpaste off their hands. Coupons were the bees' knees back in my day. Now, they're almost not even worth all the trouble."

I flick my gaze down to the bulging wallet full of coupons that sits between us. I'm glad some things never change. Aunt Suzy makes sure Kady eats, and for that I am grateful.

"How's Kady doing? Bones plays games with me. Won't let her talk to me. I thought if I could just see her... That if I could just touch her..." I trail off and turn my hardened gaze out the window.

Suzy's warm hand envelops mine and she squeezes it. "Give her some time. You've barely just gotten back. You know how she gets. Always worries over the tiniest things.

She always loved you but her heart was broken. It'll take some time to mend it. If I know my girl, she'll be warming back up to you in no time."

I let out a breath of relieved air. "Thank God. I'm not letting her go this time, Suze. I went off and got my education like she insisted. Not just any education, but one that will ensure we have a great future. I'm going to do whatever it takes to get her by my side. Once she's back where she belongs, I won't let her leave."

She turns up the dial on the radio and Otis Redding's voice blasts through the speakers. It helps ease away the last of the aches in my chest. This song, *Stand by Me*, is my sign. We're going to fix this. And Suzy is going to help me. Hell, I may even have to ask Bones for a little helping hand.

But I will get Kadence Marshall back.

"I need a favor, Suzy Q."

She blushes and grins. "Anything for you, sweetheart."

"Help me pick out a dress."

chapter three

Kady

I towel dry my hair after a much needed shower and then swipe away the steam in the mirror. I'm tired these days. So tired. Oftentimes I wonder if I could just leave. Swallow a bunch of pills and drift off quietly into nothingness.

It's always guilt that stops me though.

I couldn't do that to Agatha or Aunt Suzy. Even Bones doesn't deserve that. And my poor cat would be homeless. Where is that damn cat anyway?

"Whiskers?" I call out as I drop the towel to the floor. Completely naked, I make my way into my bedroom on a hunt for my cat that's older than dirt. When he passes on, I'm not sure how I'll cope with the loss.

Dropping to my knees, I peer under the bed to see if the orange tabby cat is hiding underneath. When I realize he's not, I groan and stand back up. It's then I notice what's on top of the bed.

"What in the world?" I mutter to myself as I snatch up

the black dress. "Aunt Suzy? Did you buy me a dress?"

She's doesn't appear to be nearby. If she were, I'd gripe at her for buying me such a nice garment. It's certainly not in the budget, not to mention I have nowhere to wear it to.

I frown when I see a chunky white necklace and a pair of black ballet flats. Both brand new. My heart rattles in my chest with worry over how much she spent this afternoon. I'm still flustered over her extravagant purchases when I see the pink note on the bed.

Yeo.

His messy scrawl on the paper scribbles its way all over my heart, marring it with his perfection. A heated blush prickles over my skin—part desire and part embarrassment. We've not seen each other in so long and now...now he wants to take me to dinner. My heart is already doing backflips with excitement. But my brain is putting on the brakes and screaming at anyone who'll listen.

Twelve years and then what?

He's back?

For good?

And he thinks we can pick right back up where we left off?

I storm away from the clothes and head toward my dresser. I'm not going to dinner with him. There's no way I can see him after all this time. My heart isn't ready. I'd probably make a fool out of myself. Turn into a blubbering mess and beg him to make love to me. *Ew, no.*

I'm about to open my top drawer when I find another note. This one is from Bones, his Zippo with a skull etched on top, holding it flat. His note is written on a paper towel.

So Bones.

Kady Baby,

The Karate Kid is back and he wants to be your baby daddy. My advice is to stay in your room. Stay far, far away from the quack doctor.

Or...

You could go to dinner with him and let him fuck you all the way into next week. If you go that route, take pictures. I need details to whack off to later.

Either way, be careful. I love you, Kady Baby.

Bones aka Badass Motherfucker aka Your Secret Boyfriend aka Big Dick

I let out a laugh and shake my head. Bones keeps me sane. If it weren't for him, I'd have lost my mind twelve years ago when I watched Mr. Anderson drive away with the love of my life.

For months I did nothing but cry.

Nobody visited me. No one dared to.

Aunt Suzy and Agatha both begged me to eat. Officer Joe even stopped by, wanting me to seek counseling. But it was Bones who made me drag my ass out of that bed. Told me I had a vagina. Vaginas were tough, he'd said. He even quoted Betty White. Where he comes up with this stuff, I'll never know.

I find some black panties and a matching bra. Despite my fear of seeing Yeo again, I'm absolutely craving everything that is him. Truth be told, I miss him terribly. By the time I finish dressing and have applied some makeup, my hair has dried into messy waves. I make quick work of braiding it into a loose side braid.

I'm beginning to panic, my thoughts drifting to Kenneth and how he copes when he panics, when a loud knock on the door resounds downstairs.

"Someone gonna get that?" I yell out.

When nobody answers, I huff and then bound down the steps. I reach the front door and take a deep breath. What if it's Norman? I should get a gun. What if it's one of Pascale's friends? Those drug addicted thugs sometimes show up on my lawn at the weirdest times. I definitely should get a gun.

"Kadence?"

All worrying thoughts about thugs and child molesters fizzle away as heat floods through me. Just the way he says my name has my heart threatening to pound right through my chest. I press my lips together into a firm line and twist the knob. When I finally see him, my heart ceases to beat.

There, standing on my front porch in all of his masculine beauty, is Yeo Anderson. He's clearly been working out because his usual tall, slender form is slightly filled out. His upper arms and chest are leaner. More defined. The white button-up shirt he dons fits him like it would a GQ model. His black tie is sleek and thin, the color matching his slacks perfectly. He wears a shiny pair of dress shoes. Clean, polished, and without a single scuff. Just like the boy himself.

Yeo looks expensive.

I don't remember him looking this expensive.

Swallowing, I flit my gaze down to my Walmart dress. I look inexpensive.

"Kadydid." His nickname for me is a whisper. I like whispers. He knows this. "You look beautiful. Even more so than I remember."

At this, I lift my eyes to meet his heated brown ones. He lifts up a dark eyebrow and smiles. Yeo's smiles are blinding and brilliant and perfect. The boy—no—the man dizzies me and confuses me whenever he's near. I can't stay locked up inside my head because he's too busy distracting me by working his way into my heart.

"It's been so long…" I trail off, tears forming in my eyes.

He takes a step forward. Then another. And then his fingertips are brushing a stray brown strand of hair away from my cheek. His touch jolts me to life. Electrifies my entire being. Resuscitates my dead soul. When he dips down, I can't help but lean in to him. To inhale his new scent. It's unfamiliar, yet still smells like him. More masculine. Older. Wiser. Yum.

"Yeo…"

And then his fingers are on me. Touching me. Owning me. Distracting me. The words I was going to say fizzle and fade as the fire that only we create rages back to life. A fire I'd assumed died after over a decade.

He was supposed to find a new life.

A new girlfriend. A wife even.

Move far the hell away from me.

Yet, here he is. His fingers curling around the back of my neck. His lips flitting over my ear, whispering secrets before brushing along my cheek, and finally crushing my own mouth. My gasp of relief is my only response—my only confirmation that what he's doing is okay—before he's kissing me like the world might end tomorrow. Hell, I'd want it to if it meant I could continue to kiss him just like this until that time.

I'm about to beg him to carry me upstairs, like old times, when he pulls away. His eyebrows are pinched together, pain screwing his face into something sad and ugly.

"Why wouldn't you see me? Why did you refuse to speak to me?" His voice is accusatory. Broken.

Emotion chokes me and I fist my hands. "You weren't supposed to come back, stupid man."

He smirks. Oh, Yeo and his perfect smirks—smirks that used to get him slapped upside the head by his mother. "I was always coming back, Kadydid."

I can't help but melt at the way he says my old nickname. A name he'd given me when I was just nine years old. When I fell head over heels in love with a ten-year-old boy and his broken camera.

"You deserve better," I try. But I don't try *too* hard. Truth is, I'm selfish. I missed him.

He laughs and I swear to God my soul rejoices. Everything about Yeo is magical and soothing. Quiet and beautiful. "I don't deserve anything. But I'll do whatever it takes to have you."

When I let out a sigh, he hugs me to him. His lips are against the top of my head and he presses a kiss there before speaking.

"I'm going to fix us. Today starts the process of making everything better. For good, my sweet Kadence."

At one time, he *had* fixed everything. My life was calm and serene. He'd been instrumental in keeping Norman away. Those assholes Pascale and Kenneth never came around as long as I was with Yeo. He protected me from the bad people in my life and loved the good ones. We'd become a team. And we were unstoppable.

Until *I* put a stop to us.

"This doesn't feel real," I tell him with a teary laugh.

He backs me up to the doorframe and presses his hips against mine. I can feel his erection poking into my stomach. "Does that feel real? Because it sure as hell feels real to me."

I stand on my toes and tilt my head back. My mouth is already missing his. It practically waters for him. "Kiss me again."

His lips hover over mine and he whispers his words against them. "I'll kiss you again and again and again until the end of time."

I let out a whimper when his tongue pushes its way into my mouth. His urgency and my neediness make for a hungry, eager kiss.

I think we might kiss for eternity when his phone blares from his pocket. He groans and reluctantly pulls away to answer it.

"What?" His frustration is evident. I flick my gaze to his slacks and can't help but smile at seeing his cock straining through his pants. God, I missed him.

He darts his eyes over to me and winks. That one action sends a thrill running through me. It chases away the despondency that always grips me and leaves sparkly Yeo remnants in its wake. When he's around, my mind is hopeful and damn near free.

Yeo is my drug.

And I willingly give my biggest vein to him to inject his

life into me.

I chew on my bottom lip while he gripes at what sounds like Dean on the other end of the line. Anxiety filters back through me, causing me to grow tense with worry. When it's just Yeo and me, it's easy to forget everything else. But just hearing his brother's raised voice on the other end of the phone is a harsh reminder that it isn't just us.

His family.

Mine…

Too many people who were pulling us apart back then when all we ever wanted was to be together.

And this is what made me force him to leave in the first place.

"We'll be there soon. Tell Dad to have a cocktail and calm the fuck down," Yeo snaps.

I jolt at his tone. Upon realizing this, he softens his features and reaches for me. Of course I grab on to his hand. How could I not? He runs his thumb over the back of my hand while he hisses whispered words to his brother. And then he hangs up.

"We just have to make an appearance is all, Kadydid. They need to know my intentions right off the bat. Then we can do whatever you want, okay? Don't let my father upset you. Please," he says softly before tugging me to him.

I know he wants me to calm down but my brain is beginning to work overtime. Scenario after scenario replays in my head of the worst possible outcomes for this dinner. All of them involve his father becoming red-faced and screaming about how I'm not good enough for Yeo. He's said it before and I know without a shadow of a doubt he'll say it again.

"Shhh," he murmurs against my hair. "We've got this, okay? Don't overthink it. I need *you*."

Twelve years is a long time to go without someone you love wholeheartedly.

But with Yeo?

It all comes rushing back.

Love. Memories. Sex. Laughter. Friendship. *Us.*

He's always been stored away in a part of my heart. I've never let him go from there, despite my attempts to physically. And from what Bones and Agatha pass on, I know he hasn't let me go either. Deep down, I knew he never would. I held on to a sliver of selfish hope in my heart no matter what my mind told me was the right thing to do. I've been Yeo's since the moment he showed up on my grandma's front lawn with his big brown eyes and crooked smile. It comforts me on a cellular level knowing that time, just a blip in the grand scheme of it all, still couldn't keep us apart.

Nodding, I swallow down my emotion as I pull away and plaster on a smile for him. "I'm here. With you. Not going to worry about what I can't control."

I'm so tired. For so long I've had to be strong. To put up walls I didn't want to erect. And Yeo crashes through them anyway. I don't have to be strong because he's strong enough for the both of us.

His brows knit together as he searches my face. Probably for my deception. Finally, after not finding any, he lets out a relieved breath. "We can do this. Together."

My mind leads me down memory lane and I gladly follow.

"We can do this," he assures me, holding my hand tight. "Together."

I want to believe him. I truly do. Yeo has never lied to me. But I'm scared.

When he senses that I'm still hesitating, he turns and gives me a lopsided grin that melts me right to the linoleum floor I stand on. "It's just you and me, Kadydid."

No teachers.

No students making fun of me.

Nobody.

Just Yeo and I.

I smooth out a non-existent wrinkle on my silky dress and give him a wobbly smile back. His hand squeezes mine again before he pushes through the gym doors and guides us into the fancily decorated room. Normally, I hate the gym. Gym class is where I receive a ton of ridicule. The teacher doesn't seem to notice or care when the other girls call me "skinny ass" or "stupid girl" or how they say Yeo is too good looking for me.

Tonight though…

Tonight it is breathtaking.

Midsummer Night's Dream is the theme. Just like Shakespeare's story we're reading in eleventh grade English class.

Trees have been made of paper mache. Glittery lights hang from every corner. The dance floor is covered with a blue, shiny covering made to look like water and colorful handmade lily pads are scattered across it.

When Yeo asked me to go to his senior prom, I'd been horrified at the idea. I didn't want people to make fun of us *dancing. Or tease me about my outfit. Their roars would have been crushing. I've seen* Carrie *by Stephen King enough to know what happens when people make fun of the weird girl at a school dance.*

But I couldn't tell him no.

He was so excited.

Went on and on about how he was going to buy me a corsage and teach me to dance. That he'd already spoken to my grandma about getting a frilly dress and getting my hair done for the event.

I just wanted to make him happy.

Turning, I chance a look at him, expecting him to be admiring the décor. Instead, I find his penetrating gaze boring into mine. All insecurities fly out the window when he looks at me as though I am his entire world. We've been through so much together in the past eight years. Surely we can get through this too.

"May I have this dance?" he asks, his eyes twinkling in a way that's more captivating than the strands of lights all around us.

A small smile breaks out on my face. Yeo makes me smile. "I'm not good at it."

He chuckles and leads me to the faux lake. "That means you're still ten times better than me, Kadydid."

Can't Help Falling in Love *by Elvis Presley starts to play around us. Everything disappears when he pulls me into his warm embrace. We aren't dancing...we're hugging and rocking. Yeo kisses me on the top of the head and strokes my bare upper back. The strapless dress feels weird but when I saw his hungry stare when he picked me up, I knew I had chosen well.*

His scent intoxicates me. A hint of his sexy cologne mixed with the lingering bit of soap. I can even smell his toothpaste. I inhale him and rest my cheek on his chest. Strong, capable hands slide to my waist, creating shivers in their wake.

My body seems to hum in response when his hot breath tickles my hair. Completely off key but so very Yeo, he sings along with the song as if the lyrics were meant for me.

"You know I love you," he murmurs. "Always. No matter what. Forever."

I swallow down my emotion and nod. He's made it clear that after I graduate, he wants to marry me. Even though spending my life with Yeo seems like the best gift I could ever receive, I can't help but feel a twinge of guilt. I would always be his burden. Always. And forever.

Lately, it's all I can think about. How I'm not enough for him. How he deserves so much more than me. One day he may want kids and I'm not even sure I could give that to him.

"Get out of your head," he says in a low tone that reminds me of a growl. He pulls away just enough so he can see me. When I don't look up at him, his finger lifts my chin. Our eyes meet and all worry bleeds away. "What are you thinking about?" he questions, a frown marring his handsome face.

I chew on my bottom lip. "The future. Where you'll be..." I trail off. "Where I'll be."

A fierce scowl forms on his face and he pulls me closer. "Our future is us. We'll be together." And then he whispers, "Forever."

This too, I want to believe.

So, for now, I do.

"I love you," I tell him, a broad smile curling my lips up.

My smiles never fail to draw out his.

And that will never change.

My memories fade but the love never does. It's always pounding hard just below the surface. With a genuine smile, I let him lead me toward his shiny, expensive car that sits next to my dull, inexpensive one and attempt to ignore Bones's irritated warning from earlier today when he found out I really was going to do this dinner.

"It'll all go to shit. Just like always, Kady Baby. Call me when it happens and I'll come save the day. Just like always."

Maybe I won't need Bones to save me this time.

Love and Yeo are all I need.

chapter four

Yeo

On the way to the restaurant, I keep my hand clasped with hers. With Kady, this is how it is. Touch her. Kiss her. Hold her. It's the only way to *keep* her. She's stubborn like that.

"Agatha posted a video on Facebook the other day. Of one of your students playing the piano. You've really found something you're good at. The girl played the song flawlessly," I tell her, cutting my eyes over to her.

Her cheeks turn pink and she grins—a look I love on her. Pride. Accomplishment. Joy. "Kyra. She's so talented. Her dad Jason is a little weird. I hate when he's the one to bring her by, but she's definitely my favorite kid to work with. Presley adores her. Sometimes they play after practice."

"Agatha posted a picture of the girls' muddy feet. She said she had to spend three hours cleaning the floors that day," I tell her with a chuckle.

She kicks off her flats and curls her feet up under her. For a moment, panic seizes me, but when she flashes me her signature Kady smile, I relax.

"I would have helped but when I came downstairs it was already clean." She shrugs her shoulders and smooths her dress over her knees. "Yeo?" Her tone turns from playful to serious. Another spike of anxiety shoots through me.

"Yeah, Kadydid?"

"Why me?"

Frowning, I turn to regard her. Her bright blue eyes, such a stark contrast to the sad soul that lurks behind them, widen at me with curiosity. I hold her gaze for a moment before focusing back on the road.

"I just knew. That first day. I've told you this before."

"So tell me again. I don't understand."

I let out a sigh as I turn into the parking lot of LeBlanc's. Once I'm parked, I turn my body to look at her. "You were so alone…"

"But I wasn't," she argues.

I laugh. "You're never alone. True. But sometimes the loneliest people are surrounded by noise. You, Kadydid, were always surrounded. Yet…" I trail off, searching for the right words, "you were sad. Something was missing and I wanted to fill it. I wanted to fill your heart with me."

She drags her face away from mine and peers out through the windshield. "You do fill my heart. But then…"

"You made me leave," I remind her.

"You weren't supposed to come back."

We're going to go round and round about this, clearly. "I did as you asked, Kady. Did Agatha tell you I got my degree? I did this for us because you asked me to. Now stop your arguing and let it happen. It was always going to happen…you just delayed the inevitable."

Her head bows to her lap and I'm afraid I'm losing her to her dark thoughts. Taking her jaw in my gentle grip, I turn her to face me. "I'm not going anywhere. You can push all you want, but I have nowhere to go but here. I'll just drag you right along with me. So give it up."

"I forgot how bossy you were," she complains, her lips quirking up into an amused smile.

"I learned it from you, if you remember correctly. I was just a quiet boy from down the street. You pulled me out of my shell and forced me to play all of your stupid girl games."

"I didn't force you." Her huff is meant to be in irritation, but I know she remembers our childhood as fondly as I do.

"You did. And paybacks are a bitch. Now, I'm forcing you to be my girlfriend again. I'm going to force you to go places with me. To kiss me. To remember us."

She sighs. "Maybe Norman will leave me alone now that you're here."

Anger surges through me and I press a soft kiss to her lips so she won't see my fury. Breathing against her lips, I vow, "The bastard won't show his face while I'm around. Pascale and Kenneth can fuck off too. Bones is debatable."

Her sweet laughter warms me through and through. "Bones is our friend. He looks after me. He looked after me when…" And just like that, her words become heavy and distant. Jesus fucking Christ she's so fragile. I'm so glad I'm home to put her back together.

"I'm here now. Bones can hang out with us as long as he wears a shirt. Nobody wants to see that shit," I tease, hoping to pull her back to me.

Her blue eyes flick to mine and brighten. "I know he owns T-shirts. I swear Aunt Suzy buys him a new one each time she goes out. All black, just like he likes them. But the damn fool never wears them. Most of them still have the tags on them."

"I'll make him wear them. Now, let's get this dinner over with so I can make love to you." I climb out of the car and saunter over to her side. When I open the door, she offers her hand to me. I pull her out and into my arms getting high on her high-pitched squeal.

As I stare at her face I missed so much, I can't help but remember the past.

"STOP TICKLING ME YEO ANDERSON!" she screams, her face turning bright red.

"Shhh," I chide with a laugh. "You'll wake up your grandma."

I've settled between her milky thighs on the sofa and have her hands pinned with one of mine. My free hand rests on her sensitive ribs. I can't help but stare at her plump pink lips. So shiny and full. Bitable. "I could stare at you all day," I tell her while grinning.

Her always troubled eyes become soft. The sudden tenderness has me releasing her hands so I can stroke her face. "So stare," she breathes, her mouth parting open.

And so I do.

I inspect her smooth forehead. It's still red, along with her cheeks, from exertion at being tickled. Her dark eyebrows match her hair perfectly and are drawn together as she watches me too. Bright blue eyes shine with love and clarity. So brilliant I'm almost blinded by it. Her pert nose flares with every ragged breath she takes. It's her lips though that I want to see more of.

Cupping her cheek, I rub my thumb along the edge of her mouth. Always so soft. I never tire of being with her.

"Am I too much for you?" she questions in a despondent tone.

I curl up my lip as if she's suddenly grown three heads. "Are you for real right now?"

She presses her sweet lips together into a firm line, her eyebrows drawing together, and nods.

Dipping down, I brush a gentle kiss to her lips. When I lift back up, she has them parted again. "Kady..."

Her nose scrunches in a cute way. "Yeah, Yeo?"

"I'll never get enough of you."

Hot breath against my neck draws me from my memory. "I'm nervous." Jesus, I've missed this girl. When we're together, it's just easy. The staying apart was what was difficult.

"I'm nervous too. It won't be easy," I say with a sigh and squeeze her to me. "But that's okay. Nothing ever worth having was easy. If things get too uncomfortable in there, we'll bail."

She nods and I reluctantly release her. I grab my jacket from the backseat and shrug it on knowing Dad will have a fit if I'm not dressed to impress. Threading her fingers with mine, I take a deep breath to fortify myself against the shit storm we'll no doubt encounter. Earlier, Dean called and went fucking ballistic on me over the phone. *You know how Dad feels about her*, he'd said. *He's going to flip when she shows up*, he'd threatened. And I pretty much told him to go fuck himself because I didn't care.

I don't care.

But I know she does.

That's where shit gets tricky.

"I feel like no time was lost," she murmurs, mostly to herself as we approach the glass doors to the front of the brick building.

"You know I've always been there for you, Kadydid. Checking up on you. Sneaking glimpses of you. Worrying my head to the point of insanity over you. Just because you didn't see me that often doesn't mean I wasn't there for you."

She flashes me a shy smile. "Agatha told me. Sometimes I'd sneak on her Facebook to check up on you too. Why didn't you ever date anyone?"

I stop before we enter the building and turn toward her. Tracing my fingertip along her jaw, I furrow my eyebrows together and regard her. Her blue eyes are clear—the storm that used to brew in them is temporarily calm. The lips I'd missed for far too long are plump and slightly parted. With each breath she takes, her nostrils flare slightly. If it were up to me, I'd freeze this moment so I could stare at her for years and years and years. Uninterrupted. Easy. Mine.

"It's only ever been you, Kady, who had my heart. You know this. Did you date anyone?" I question. I already know the answer but I ask anyway.

"No."

I dip down and kiss her lips.

Her murmured words against my mouth send a thrill of excitement coursing through me. "But surely you slept with someone while you were there. That's a long time for a man and—" I silence her with a deeper kiss, reveling in the minty fresh taste on her tongue. When I finally break from our kiss, she's panting and I'm sporting a big-ass hard-on.

"If my hand counts, then yes," I say, offering her a smoldering grin at which she giggles. "But to be honest, I was intensely focused on my studies. Then, my internship stole all of my time. Even if I'd wanted to—which I didn't—I had no time to date or fuck around. Bones can attest to this." I swallow down my unease and pin her with a firm, loving stare. "When my head finally did hit the pillow, you were on my mind. Always."

Her shoulders seem to relax at my words and her lips quirk up on one side. "He did keep me in the know. I thought about you too. Always."

Clutching her hand, I guide her inside the dark restaurant. "No more thinking or longing or wishing. We're together now."

I feel impenetrable with her in my grip. Dad will play his games. But it doesn't matter anymore. Kady is my other half—always has been, always will be—and now that my internship is out of the way, we can carry on with our life together.

"There he is," Barclay booms from one corner of the restaurant. He saunters over to us, all six feet and five inches of him, a gigantic grin on his face that looks so much like Dad's, it's spooky. "Man of the hour. Dr. Froot Loop."

I bristle at his comment but thankfully Kadence doesn't

seem to catch on. "Barc. Long time no see."

Pulling my hand from hers, I offer it to my brother for a brief handshake that turns into one of those manly half-hugs with a shoulder slap. As soon as our display of affection is over, my hand is back in hers.

"Miss Kadence. How are you these days?" His smile is forced but at least he's trying. More than I can say for the rest of my family.

She drops her gaze to the floor, her anxiety thick and clouding the air around her. "Fine. Busy."

His eyes flicker to mine and I shake my head. "How's business?"

He launches into an animated recount of his latest "piss-ant" client. How Dean ended up taking the fucker because he was about to run his fist through his nose. I try not to roll my eyes at his over-exaggerated tale. My gut tells me he wants Dad to be the proudest of him. And truth be told, Dad *is* the proudest of him. But it doesn't keep him from always trying to hold that title. Neither Dean nor I are fighting for the crown, though, so I'm not sure why he wastes all of his energy doing so.

"Come on. Everyone's waiting," he finally says and leads the way through the restaurant to a long table by the windows that overlook the Monongahela River.

Everyone is present and accounted for. Dad heads up one end of the table, his chiseled jaw set with concentration as he listens to Evelyn gab at his left. Mom, her black hair tied into a neat bun, listens intently as well at his right. Beside Mom is Larnie, the older twin, who stares at her phone and beside her Lacey, the youngest, who also stares at her phone. Both girls have light brown hair straightened to perfection, a spitting image of their mother Patty. Patty attempts to chat with a younger woman with silky red hair who sits between her and Dean. I'm presuming the redhead is his newest girlfriend. Dean's arm is slung over the chair behind her and he visually feasts on her tits spilling out of her dress as the two women converse.

As if they all realize we're here at exactly the same time, the table grows quiet and they all look over at us. They go from laughing and chatting to frowning. Kady's palm grows clammy in mine and I become overwrought with worry about this dinner. It'd been my intention to barge in here with her on my arm, basically tell them all to fuck off in the nicest way possible, and then carry on without another care in the world. I should have known it wouldn't be so easy.

Dad stands and his hardened gaze skips over me to disdainfully take in the appearance of my Kady. Evelyn reaches a hand up to calm him—something I've seen her do often over the years. But he doesn't calm. His jaw ticks as he clenches it and a muscle in his neck tightens. It's my mother who actually settles his storm, though.

"Oh, Fletcher," she says to him as she stands beside him. "Our boy is officially a doctor now. And look at Miss Kadence. What a handsome couple they are." Her English is perfect, something she worked at diligently over the last thirty years, but her accent remains thick.

Dad softens at her tone and nods once—clipped and irritated—before striding over to me. He's never been affectionate with my brothers, but for some reason he babies me, even as I stand nearly as tall and every bit as broad as him. I'm tugged from Kadence's grip and smashed into one of his bear hugs. "I'm so proud of you, son."

When he releases me, I attempt to snatch Kady's hand in mine but Patty is already ushering her over to meet the redhead. It should comfort me that they are trying to make her feel welcome, but it doesn't. I promised her I'd keep her by my side.

"Ja-gi-ya," Mom coos and pulls me into a hug. She's tiny and nearly half my size. "Don't fuss about your father. He'll come around." We had a long discussion today over lunch about what my father's reaction would be about my decision to make Kady a part of my life again.

My eyes flit over to Kady and her arms are crossed over her chest. A signature defense move of hers. It makes me straighten. "I hope so."

Releasing my mother, I hurry over to Kady and pull her against my chest. Her body is tense but she relaxes against me. "I'm here now, Kadydid. Let's get some food into you."

"They hate me," she murmurs.

I stroke her long brown hair and shake my head. "Nobody could ever hate you."

chapter five

Kady

He's wrong.

    I hate me.

And they *definitely* hate me.

He is one of the few people who *don't* hate me.

I can sense the distrust in their eyes. The worry of how this little poor girl will embarrass them in their big affluent world. And I will. It's just how I am. At some point tonight, no matter how hard I try not to, I'll make a fool out of myself and everyone here.

Yeo knows this and yet he doesn't care.

Which makes my heart bleed.

He should have stayed away.

Dinner has gone smoothly so far, thank God. With Yeo's constant touch, he distracts me. His soothing presence helps me focus on him and not everything around me. Everything in me. Everything about me.

"What are you doing these days, Kadence?" Patty

questions.

I jolt at her words and my eyes fly to her pretty green ones. Her smile is forced and I hate that she has to pretend to be nice to me. At least Fletcher doesn't pretend. He may by Yeo's asshole father, but I know where I stand with him. Always. And that place is pretty much along the lines of dirt on the bottom of his expensive loafers.

Their eyes are all on me, waiting for me to answer. But my tongue is sticky in my mouth. I reach for my now empty wine glass and opt for the full glass of water instead. Once I've gulped down half the glass, I dart my eyes from Fletcher back to Patty. "Stuff."

One of the twins snickers at my comment and a heated blush creeps up my neck. Yeo leans in, presses a soft kiss to my cheek, and whispers, "Relax. Tell them about Kyra."

At this, I do let go of some of the tension in my shoulders. "Um, I've been teaching piano to some neighborhood kids. Kyra is my star student. Has an ear for music and responds well to my critiques." I chew on my lip and shoot Yeo a nervous glance. His warm, chocolate eyes twinkle with adoration which gives me the strength I need to continue. "Business has picked up. I'm teaching nearly every evening but now that summer is here, I'll most likely fill the days up instead. Thanks, um, for asking, Patty."

This time, she actually smiles at me. Her real smiles are pretty.

"I've tried to talk the girls into getting some lessons before they go off to college but—"

"Mom, ew. No." Lacey's lip curls up in disgust and she shoots Larnie a secretive look only twins can interpret.

"Put the phones away," Barclay orders with a growl before turning his scrutinizing gaze on me. "Brennan said he saw you over on Fifth Street last week. Nothing but drug dealers and whores out that way. Not a safe part of town for a nice young lady."

Yeo stiffens from beside me and I panic. The napkin in my lap suffers at my abuse as I twist and tug at it, unsuccessfully attempting to rip the fabric in half. "I didn't go to Fifth Street. Besides, Officer Joe told me it's a bad part of town. I stay mostly at the house."

Barclay shrugs as if he didn't just accuse me of something awful. "Who is this Joe you speak of? Brennan's been a detective for three years there and I've never heard him mention him."

I frown at him. Officer Joe is the best cop in Morgantown. It was him who promised me everything would be okay. That he'd look after me no matter what.

"Officer Joe works in another department," Yeo says, his teeth clenched together as he speaks. "Brennan is an idiot. Back the hell up, man." His warning to his brother is loud and clear. Barclay laughs and then launches into an animated story about how a new hotel is breaking dirt in a few weeks. Apparently he's a part owner. Apparently he'll hook everyone up with a night in the penthouse suite. Apparently they've named it after him.

I stifle a giggle remembering what Bones said once about Barclay. *"The man's so worried about pleasing his daddy that he lives up to his name."* He starts barking obnoxiously like a dog. *"Bark!"* Then he coos. *"Laaaaaay."* It had gotten me through an embarrassing moment when I'd showed up at Yeo's as a teenager looking for him. Barclay had called me all sorts of names and ridiculed me. When I ran back home crying, it was Bones who came up with insult after insult about Yeo's brother that ended up turning my tears into uncontrollable laughter.

I wish Bones were here now.

He'd know exactly what to say.

How to deal with Barclay.

"Well," Fletcher announces and rubs at his stomach before reaching for his wine glass. "Now that we've made it through dinner without incident"—his eyes cut to mine before landing on Yeo—"I just wanted to congratulate my youngest boy on his accomplishments. Yeo, your family is proud of you. We've never had a doctor in the family before, and I know everyone is incredibly happy. I'd tossed the idea around back and forth with your mother, and we decided instead of a house or a car or money, we'd gift you a building for your achievement. You've let it be known that you'd like to open a private practice. We want to aid in your endeavors. So next week, we'll head out together and find something that'll suit your needs. We're glad to have you home, son."

He raises his glass and everyone follows. I raise my half-empty water glass with a shaky hand.

"To Dr. Anderson. May he help all of the quacky ducks in Morgantown," Dean blurts out, his voice loud and slightly slurred. Elena, his girlfriend, frowns at his toast before cutting her eyes apologetically over to mine.

The twins start snickering under their breath. I drop my gaze to my barely touched food and try to drown out their voices. Evelyn and Patty both scold them. Yeo is snapping at his brother, words spoken so harsh and quick I don't even pick up on them. I can feel Fletcher's penetrating gaze dissecting me. Bile rises in my throat, causing me to jerk my hand from Yeo's.

"I, ·uh, I..." I trail off as I stand on wobbly legs. Everything around me darkens. All I can think about is getting away from this table. Away from their ridicule and disdainful glares. "An emergency came up at home. I need to leave."

Not waiting for anyone's permission, I bolt, digging in my purse along the way. I need Bones. He'll get me the hell out of here. When I find my phone, I clutch it in my grip as I push out of the chilly restaurant and suck in deep, cleansing breaths of the warm late spring night.

I'm attempting to find my center. To calm the hell down but the opposite happens. Memories consume me. They claw at me and drag me down into their fiery depths of the abyss.

I wake from a nightmare and my skin feels cold. But it's sticky and wet. It's then I realize I awoke from shouts, not a nightmare. Mommy and Daddy are arguing in the living room. Every word can be heard through the paper thin walls. My palms go to my ears and I attempt to smash away their sounds. Sounds of glass breaking. Crying and screaming. Cussing.

"Twinkle, twinkle, little star..." I whisper as I try and

drown out their roars. "How I wonder what you—"

"YOU'RE A FUCKING WHORE!" *Daddy screams just outside my door.*

I jump and scramble to the head of my bed before dragging my blanket up to my chin. When I asked my babysitter what a fucking whore was last week, she yanked me up by my elbow and spanked me. I was confused as to why I was in trouble. All I wanted to know is why Daddy calls Mommy that all the time.

"Norman," *Mommy begs,* "you'll wake Kadence. Shhh."

Mommy doesn't know I'm already awake. I wish Daddy would be quiet, though. I don't like when he yells at her and calls her mean names.

"Maybe she needs to know what a whore you are!" *he roars.* "She'll probably grow up to be just like you. Spreading her legs to half the goddamned neighborhood. Is she even fucking mine?"

Mommy sobs and I shiver.

"Of course she's yours. You see the way she...you know that..." *she trails off.*

"That she's fucked in the head just like me?" *he says with a hateful laugh.* "Of course she is! We have to live with you! Your bullshit makes us crazy fucking mad!"

"No!" *Mommy argues.*

Everything goes silent when I hear a crunch. And then an ear-piercing wail. "I'm bleeding!"

Bravery I didn't know I possessed has me scrambling off my bed and out my bedroom door. Mommy is on her knees in the living room, her nightgown half torn from her shaking body showing her booby. Daddy stands over her, his hands fisted as he breathes heavily like a monster. Blood covers Mommy's hands. Her frantic eyes meet mine. It's almost like she has a superpower and is silently telling me to go back into my room. I can feel her words inside my head. Go, baby. Go back to bed. *But I don't go. Instead, I run toward Daddy and tug at his wrist.*

"Daddy, Mommy is bleeding," *I tell him, fat tears welling in my eyes.*

His head snaps over to glare down at me. He's never looked so scary before. I can smell his stinky beer scent mixed with sweat. It makes me feel like puking.

"Are you a whore like Mommy?" *he taunts, his lip curling up as if he thinks I'm disgusting. My heart aches at the look on his face.*

"What's a whore?"

Mommy cries some more but my eyes are locked on my daddy's angry ones. He sits down on the sofa in front of Mommy and grabs a handful of her hair. When he turns her head to face me, he spits out his words. "This is a whore. Are you a whore, Kady?"

I look at Mommy's pretty blue eyes that are red from crying. Her hair is dark and messy like mine. Everyone says I look just like her. "Yes, Daddy. I'm a whore like Mommy." *I lift my chin bravely at him.*

His eyes flicker the way the neighbor's pit bull Butch does when I sneak him bacon leftover from breakfast. Hungry. Starved. Scary almost. At least a fence is always there to separate me from Butch. There's no fence between me and Daddy.

"That's what I thought," *he slurs.* "Go get the first aid kit and bring it here." *His voice softens and I pray he's going to stop being mean to Mommy. I run from him. Once I've located the kit, I scurry back into the living room where Mommy still kneels in front of Daddy.*

"Come sit in my lap and fix up your whore mother," he instructs, patting at his thigh.

Mommy starts crying harder, shaking her head, but I beam at her. This time, I'm the one with secret powers. I tell her in my mind that I can fix her and Daddy. When I crawl into his lap, he situates me to where I face her. He strokes my hair gently while I play doctor on Mommy.

I look over my shoulder to smile at Daddy who smiles back.

See, I fixed it.

Turning back to Mommy, I finish making her all better.

I made everyone happy.

When the memory dissipates, I feel slightly disoriented. It takes a moment to realize I'm standing in front of the steakhouse waiting for my ride out of here. My entire body shudders as the past lingers heavily in the air. I miss my mom so much. She was sweet and beautiful. Too young to leave this world. My mother wasn't even as old as I am now before she left me. A burning ache surges through me and clutches at my heart.

Fucking Norman.

As if just thinking about him might suddenly make him materialize, I shudder away any impending thought of him. Instead, I try to think about things that make me happy.

Yeo.

Piano.

Presley and Agatha and Bones and Aunt Suzy and Officer Joe.

Whiskers.

Rainbow-flavored snow cones.

Beethoven and Justin Timberlake.

"Get out of here, Kady Baby. I'll let Yeo know you've gone," Bones assures me, his voice calming me down. "And don't you worry about Norman. The moment I get ahold of his ass, I'll gut him. That's a motherfucking promise."

Bones may be a flake most days but when he makes a "motherfucking promise," I know he won't stop until he makes good on said promise.

I don't even turn around to thank him before I make my escape.

chapter six

Yeo
Ten years old

The moving truck is backed up to the old grey house and curiosity is killing me. Mom told me to leave them alone—whoever they are—but I can't. I have to know if the new people have any kids to play with. Sometimes I play with Jake next door, but he's closer to Barclay's age. Whenever Dad brings Barclay and Dean over, Jake tries to act older and sides with my brothers instead of me. It annoys me that he's too good to play with me when they're around.

A car honks at me and I swerve out of the street. My tire hits the curb, which causes me to fly off my bike and into the grass in front of the grey house. It's the biggest house on our street, but it's also the ugliest. Sometimes I hear someone playing music. When I'm being bad, Mom threatens to sign me up for piano lessons with the old lady who lives there. So far I've been able to talk my way out of it every time.

I sit up on my knees and inspect the scrape on my elbow. It stings but it doesn't dampen my curiosity any. I'm dying to know who's moving into this house. I wait for what seems like hours for any sign of kid life. I've almost given up when I see *her*.

Long dark hair swept away from her face in a white headband. Wide blue eyes that seem sad. An almost fragile looking, tiny body. Worry surrounds me as I wonder if a breeze would take the girl who seems to be around my age and blow her right away from me.

With a grunt, I climb to my feet and dust off my knees with my palms. The girl plops down on the bottom step as movers carry furniture into the house. Her jeans have holes in the knees and her T-shirt looks three sizes too big. If my brothers were here, they'd probably tease her and call her a boy. The thought makes me angry. I quickly push it away.

"Hi."

Her bright eyes lift and find mine. They don't flicker and shine with playfulness like I'm used to seeing from most kids our age. Instead, they hide secrets. Secrets I decide right then I'll do anything to discover. "Hi."

I run my dirty palm through my hair and attempt a smile. But she's not smiling which makes me unhappy. I'm dying to know if her eyes shine when she smiles.

"I'm Yeo."

Her lips twitch and I give myself a mental high-five for almost making her smile.

"I'm Kady."

"Like a katydid?"

She scrunches her nose up in a cute way. "What's a katydid?"

"A bug. It imitates things like leaves. I did a report on it in the third grade."

Her eyes narrow and she regards me thoughtfully. "I can imitate my new cat, Whiskers. My friend gave him to me," she boasts and then crawls on her hands in knees in front of me. "MEOOOOOW."

I laugh. "Your cat sounds awful."

"He's not awful." She pouts. "He's a sweet orange and black tabby cat. Want to meet him?"

Shaking my head, I hold my palms up to her. "I'm allergic to cats."

"MEOOOOOW," she mewls and nuzzles her head against my knee.

I reach down and pet her soft hair. "You're a strange girl, Kadydid."

She stands up and grins a toothy smile at me. I'm taller than her by several inches but I like that she's smaller than me. I feel big and strong beside her. Like I could be her protector.

"You're strange too. Are you Chinese? Grandma sometimes takes us to a Chinese restaurant where they give us fortune cookies. Last time my fortune said, 'Keep your eye out for someone special.' Are you special?" she questions, her nose doing that cute scrunching thing again.

"Not really. I was born in Seoul, South Korea. I'm not Chinese. There's a difference," I tell her with a raised eyebrow. I'm trying to impress her but I'm not sure I even know what the difference is between being Chinese and

Korean. Only what Mom tries to teach me of my birthplace and heritage. Half the time I'm too eager to go ride my bike or pester Barclay to care about listening as she goes on about the Gyeongbokgung Palace or the time she took Dad to The Korean War Museum where he made a fool of himself trying to speak Korean. And failing horribly, the way she tells it. I'd always listened with one ear but had been distracted by everything else. Now, I wish I'd paid more attention. For Kady.

"Sounds special. I was born here in Morgantown. I'm not special." Her eyes fall to my *Star Wars* shirt and I suddenly feel embarrassed. My brothers wear cologne and nice shirts. Dean even drives now. I feel stupid under her gaze.

"*I'm* not special," I assure her. Then, I lift her chin with my finger so I can see her sad eyes again. "I certainly can't meow like a cat from hell."

She giggles and pushes me away. "Bones would like you. He says bad words too."

"Is Bones your dog?"

At this she cackles and dramatically rolls in the grass beside the walkway clutching her stomach. "He'd be so mad if he knew you thought he was a dog!" Her howling laughter makes me laugh too.

"Is he your brother?"

She sits with her legs crossed and picks a long blade of grass. "He's like a brother, yeah."

My smile grows knowing I've gained not one friend but two. I don't need Jake anymore. I have Kady and Bones.

"Bones!" she yells toward the house.

I look up and an older woman, probably Kady's mom,

stares at me. Her lips are drawn down into a frown. She has a black eye, like the one Dean got that time Barclay punched him for making out with his girlfriend. It's purple and swollen and ugly. The woman swallows and then retreats back into the house.

Kady stands and shields her eyes against the sun as she peers up at the house. "Maybe he's begging my grandma for a snack. This is weird. He always comes when I call for him." She turns her head back to look at me. She chews on her bottom lip while she mulls over his nonresponse.

"Maybe next time I come over I'll bring some tteok since he likes snacks. They're yummy. Way better than dumb fortune cookies," I tell her with a grin.

Her eyes twinkle in the sunlight and I decide right then that she's going to be my best friend. I like looking at her pretty eyes and sad smiles. I hope her sort-of brother likes me too.

"What is tteok?"

"Kinda like rice cakes."

She makes a pretend gagging noise. "Gross! Bones will most definitely not like that. He likes Cheetos. Bring those."

"Deal."

It's rained for three days straight. I'm dying to go back over to Kady's and meet Bones. But Mom won't let me ride my bike in the rain.

"Why don't you invite Jake over to play video games?" Mom questions, sipping her hot tea, the smell of lemon and honey filling the air.

I groan but don't leave my perch by the front window where I can just see Kady's front yard. "I don't want to play with him. Plus, he likes Barclay better than me anyway."

Dad's paper rustles from behind me and he clears his throat. "Yeo, come here."

With a sigh that I don't let Dad hear, I stand and walk over to him. He pats his knee and I sit in his lap. It's a good thing Barclay and Dean are with their Mom today or else they'd tease me. They always say I'm Dad's "baby."

"What's got you down, son?"

He hugs me to him and I frown. "I met a new friend. Her name's Kady. It's rained every day and I want to play with her."

His body stiffens at my words which causes me to look up at him in question. He scowls before barking out his words. "Norman and Louise's kid?"

I shrug my shoulders. "I don't know."

He cuts his eyes over to Mom and gives her a slight shake of his head before turning back to me. "Does Kady live in the grey house down the street?"

I nod.

"I don't want you going over there. Do you understand me?"

At this, I jerk my head over to Mom and plead with her. "What? Why not? Mom, tell him Kady's nice."

Her gaze falls to her tea and she sips it. "Listen to your father."

Angry tears well in my eyes, and I slide out of his lap. "You're a mean dad!"

Rushing from the living room, I leave my parents behind as they argue in hushed tones. When I get to my room, I slam the door and dramatically fall onto my bed face first. Why would Dad tell me not to play with Kady? What could possibly be bad about a girl with pretty eyes and a sad smile?

I'm crying hot, angry tears when I hear the door open and close. I know it's Mom because she smells like ginger. Her comforting scent only makes me cry harder. She pulls up my desk chair to my bed and pats my back.

"Your dad knows things you don't know, Yeo. He's wise."

I sniffle and shake my head. "Not about this, Mom."

She's silent for a bit while she strokes my back. "Ja-gi-ya," she says after some time, "you're a smart boy. I trust your judgment. If you say the girl is good, then she's good. Always be careful, though. I'm afraid Dad's more worried about her parents than her. Norman isn't nice like your dad. It's not okay for you to play there if Norman is home. Can you at least promise me that?"

Rolling over to my side, I look at my mother. She's smart and beautiful. I can see why my dad picked her to be his wife. "So I can play with her? Right now?"

She grins at me. "Yep. Just make sure your behind is home by dinner."

Mom doesn't have to tell me twice before I'm bounding down the stairs, making a quick pass through the kitchen, and running into the rain without another look back. She calls out for me to grab an umbrella but I'm too excited.

"Is Kady home?"

I'm soaked to the bone which means Mom will be up-set at me for not listening and running out into the rain without the umbrella. I probably look like a drowned rat. The lady with the black eye doesn't look any better. In fact, she looks like she might break at any moment. She's pretty but not like my mom. She doesn't look smart like my mom either. This lady looks lost and confused. Messy and lonely.

"Uh," she looks over her shoulder before glancing back down at me. "She's not feeling so well at the moment."

"Can Bones play then?" I question holding up a bag of Cheetos. "I brought his favorite."

Tears well in her eyes and they spill down her cheeks. "You want to play with him? You're not afraid of him?"

"Why would I be afraid of him?"

She swallows and waves me into the house. For a mo-ment I worry about my allergies to their cat but am thank-ful I'm not bothered right away. Maybe it's an outside cat. Poor thing…it's pouring outside.

I sit down on the sofa while the woman wanders off somewhere in the house. A few moments later, footsteps bound down the stairs. I see a flash of skin and dark hair as a kid runs by. Then, my Cheetos are stolen right from my grasp.

"These are for me. Kady said you'd be back."

I gape at the kid who runs by in nothing but a pair of underwear.

"I'm Bones."

Bones lives up to the name. Rib bones protruding out. Nothing but knobby knees and elbows. Bruises mar the kid's pale midsection. It makes me angry. Is Norman responsible for these bruises?

"I'm Yeo. But you already know that..."

"Yep, Kady told me. She said you were cute, but I don't see it. Kind of fugly if you ask me. Why does your hair stick up? Your eyes look weird. Do you eat cats? Kady will kill you if you eat her cat. Just sayin.'"

Before I can respond, an older woman walks in and smiles at me. "You must be Fletcher and Gyeong's boy. Yeo is it? Your mother approached me about possibly taking some piano lessons this summer. I'm Ruth."

I give her a polite smile. "Yeah, it's Yeo. Nice to meet you."

She sits down in the armchair and regards me, her grey eyebrows bunching together. "I see you've met my granddaughter's friend Bones. He's a troublemaker but we love him anyway."

He rewards her by dropping a handful of Cheetos into her palm. "Yeo eats cats. Poor Whiskers," he whispers loud enough for me to hear.

My skin heats at his words and I shake my head at her. "I swear, Miss Ruth, I don't eat cats."

She chuckles. "Bones likes to fib. Don't mind him. So you're here to see Kady, huh?"

I dart my gaze over to Bones who is now sucking cheesy remnants from each finger before giving up and wiping them on the couch. My mom would throw a fit if I did that. Cringing, I turn to look at the old lady.

"Should I go?"

Her features become more wrinkled when she frowns.

I don't like how sad she looks. Everyone in this house is sad. It makes me sad too.

"I think if you could stay for a bit, Kady might feel well enough to see you. Can you stay for her?"

Bones drags out a Chutes 'N Ladders game. Each piece gets stained with Cheetos' goo as he sets it up. "I'll go first since I'm the coolest. If Kady were here she could go next. She's almost as cool as me but waaaaaaaaay cooler than you. Since she's not here, you can go after me."

I frown and shoot Ruth a questioning stare. She simply smiles at me.

"Boom!" Bones yells, making my ears hurt. "Beat that, Kitty Muncher."

Groaning, I spin the wheel to take my turn.

My new friends are strange.

They're still better than Barclay's butt kisser Jake though...

chapter seven

Yeo
Present

By the time I untangle myself from Mom and Dad's concerned lecture and make it outside, it's too late. She's gone.

I sigh when I see Bones leaned up against the wall puffing on a cigarette. At least he's dressed and at least he's not smoking pot. Small victories.

"Where's Kady?"

He shrugs and starts walking toward the parking lot, clutching the purse Kady left behind awkwardly in his grip. "Home."

Following after him, I curse myself at how I let things get so out of hand. Bringing her here was a mistake. She and I have always done best when it's just us two. Everyone else only complicates things.

"Need a lift back to the house?" I ask.

He stops sauntering away from me and turns to look

my way. "They attacked her, man. That's what your family does. Attack."

Flinching at his words, I can't help but agree. "I know. I'm sorry. I should have known better."

For once he isn't doling out his bullshit. He looks hurt too. I'm fucking up all over the place today.

"Why'd you come back? She was happy, goddammit," he growls.

Running my fingers through my hair, I grumble in frustration. "The plan was always to come back, Bones. We both know this."

His gaze bores a hole through me for a long minute before he shakes away his anger. "Where's your car? I'm hot as fuck. I'm about to take this shit off." When he motions to his clothes, I cringe. If my dad got a look at Bones stripping down in the parking lot of his favorite steakhouse, he'd have a coronary. I may be a doctor but I'm not *that* kind of doctor.

"The black one," I point behind him. "There."

He strides over to it and yanks open the passenger door. I'm thankful it's dark out because he does the inevitable and yanks the material over his head before tossing it into the car. I rush over to the vehicle to climb inside before anyone sees. Once I've started the car and the air conditioning is blowing, he turns to look at me. My gaze falls to his newest tattoo that encircles his nipple and I shake my head. When I meet his stare again, he's watching me with interest.

"You like it?"

I clench my teeth together and nod. That's the only answer I can give him. Putting the car into drive, I peel out of my parking spot and cruise out of the parking lot before my family can see my undisciplined friend.

"I got it for you," he says, fumbling with his Zippo as he looks out the window.

"Thanks."

The car ride is quiet. I'm not going to acknowledge the fact that Bones has my name tattooed over and over again in an infinite loop around his nipple. He wants to get a rise out of me. But I'm on to his game.

I'm lost in thought when a hand roughly grabs my dick. I nearly lose control of the wheel and send him a murderous glare. "What the fuck, man? Get your hand off my cock."

He grins and winks at me but doesn't let go. "Your cock likes me. Or did you forget?"

With an annoyed growl, I shove his hand away from me. "That was a long time ago."

"Old enough to know better, but still too young to care?"

Always fucking riddles with this guy. "Whatever, man."

"She was never mad about those times, you know. It turned her on," he taunts. "I know she flipped the bean one too many times with those images on her mind. Told me so herself…"

I clench my teeth and try to drive away all images of those nights. Nights where Bones and I got piss-assed drunk. Nights where he coaxed me into a lot of things I regretted the next day. Nights where he filled a void when Kady refused to see me.

When his hand clutches my dick again, I pull the damn car over and shove it into park. I grip his wrist to yank it away, but before I do, our eyes meet. Hurt flashes in his blue orbs that has me taking pause.

"What are you doing, Bones?"

"She leaves you wanting all the time," he mutters thoughtfully. "Then she mopes around the house longing for you. That shit creeps up on a crazy fuck like me. Seeps its way into my bones. She's got me feeling all kinds of needy for you too. What'd ya say, kimchi boy, wanna let Bones take care of that eager cock?"

This time I do shove him away. "Enough. You're pissing me off."

He shrugs and kicks his now bare feet up on the dash. "Your loss. You know where I live."

The air is charged with confusion the entire way back to the house. Neither of us speak. And the moment we pull into the driveway, he jumps out and disappears inside the house. I sit in the car for a few minutes to collect myself. No matter what I do, I seem to always say and do the wrong things. I'm fucked in every direction.

Nothing is going at all how I planned for it to go.

I'm just climbing out of the car to apologize to Bones when that asshole Pascale saunters out of the house. I know it's him because I recognize his fucking beanie he wears on his head even in the dead of summer. He's wearing a pair of loose shorts and a white tank that shows his tattoos beneath. I hate the guy with a passion.

"What the fuck are you doing here?" I snarl and charge for him.

He smirks upon seeing me and reaches behind him, no doubt going for his gun, but I've already tackled him into the grass. We grunt and wrestle but I'm bigger. I wrangle the gun out of his hand, tossing it far away from him. He spits at me. "Get off me, fuckin' prick!"

I hold his forearms into the earth and glower at him. "Why are you here?"

"I was just leaving."

"Does Kady know you were here?"

He attempts to spit at me again but I clutch his throat, giving it a tight squeeze. I thought I ran him off long ago. Time to be a dick and remind him why he's not welcome.

"You're not allowed in her home. Officer Joe said the next time you come around—"

"FUCK OFFICER JOE!"

I tighten my grip around his throat until he stops squirming. When his tongue hangs out just a bit, I get right in his face. "Don't fucking come here again or I'll have you locked up."

When I release him, he laughs. "For what? Selling weed?"

"You're trash, Pascale. You and I both know you do more than sell weed. Agatha says you've been known to deal cocaine."

He rolls out from beneath me and scrambles to his feet. We both eye the gun in the yard but he wisely doesn't try to go after it. "I oughta cut that bitch for talkin' shit about me—"

Charging for him, I grab the front of his shirt and snarl at him. "You touch one goddamned hair on her head and I'll end you. Fucking end you."

When I let him go and he disappears into the darkness,

I find the gun and lock it in my car before going inside. The house is quiet. Bones is pissed at me. Kady is upset. I can't win today. Defeated, I shed my jacket and climb the stairs. Finding Kadence's room, I lose my tie and shirt before kicking off my shoes and climbing into her empty bed.

Where are you, Kadydid?

I wake to Whiskers sitting on my chest staring at me. His eyes are narrowed and knowing. The only damn cat I'm not allergic to. Who knew?

"Hey, kitty," I coo, and stroke his head. "Missed you."

He purrs and digs his claws into my chest. His meows are cute. This cat may be old but he's still playful like a kitten.

"You hungry? Anyone feed you lately?"

His meow is needy and pitiful. I scoop him in my arms to carry him downstairs. He's the fattest cat I've ever seen. When we make it into the kitchen, I find his bowl and then pour some milk into it. I microwave it for a few seconds to warm it before setting it on the counter. Whiskers hops onto the countertop with ease and laps at his milk. While he drinks, I scratch his back. He finishes and nuzzles against my hand. I know the drill. Scooping his heavy ass back into my arms, I take him over to the couch.

My thoughts are on Kady as I pet his head. I drift off with the girl of my dreams on my mind.

"You smell like Whiskers."

I yawn and squint in the darkness. I'm not sure how

long I was out for. Someone has turned off all the lights and the cat is long gone.

"Where you been, Kadydid?"

She lets out a sad sigh. I can't see her in the dark but I can feel her. Kady is more than a sight, she's a force of nature. I want her to obliterate me.

"Out and about. Been thinking." Even though she attempts to keep her tone light, I sense her upcoming descent into her depression hell. It's in her voice. A crack. A tiny tell that only I would notice. She can't hide those parts of herself from me. I've studied every single aspect about her. One tip in the wrong direction and she will plummet into the darkness. Kady belongs in the light.

I stand and seek her out. She's avoiding my touch but at least she's talking to me. When I hear a creak of the stairs, I dart in that direction. She's quick and bounds up the steps just out of reach. Always running. Always hiding.

But I always find her.

I always catch her.

"Kadence, come here."

The door to her bedroom squeaks and I pad softly in after her.

"I'm no good for you."

Prowling through the darkness, I seek her out on her scent alone. Sweet and pure. Mine. Her small ragged gasps give her away. A moment later, I have her in my arms. So sweet.

"You're the only one for me," I whisper against her hair.

Her small arms wrap around my waist and she hugs me tight. All of the chaos that surrounds this broken woman is worth it if it means having moments like this. Sliding my hand up the side of her neck, I lift her chin with my thumb. I brush a soft kiss against her lips. A small whimper escapes her and I want to fucking devour it.

"Yeo, I'm so sorry. For everything…"

I chuckle and suck her bottom lip into my mouth. She tastes like the best dessert, the sweetest tea, the most savory steak. Delicious. I'll crave her until I die. "You'll never have anything to be sorry for. When you run from me, I get lost and confused. But when you let me catch you, you make me happy again. Stop running, Kadydid. Stay with me. Always."

My palm travels along her throat to her breast. Her breath catches when my thumb skims over her hardened nipple. That small sound works magic on my cock and it's suddenly alive. So damn alive. And needy. Needy to take her over and over until the sun comes up.

We can fix this.

She doesn't argue when I grab the hem of her shirt and peel it from her body. Kady doesn't fool with bras much and I'm always thankful for less barriers between us.

My eyes close when her fingers work urgently at the buckle of my pants. Our mouths meet again, this time fiery and passionate. The moment her small hand has a grip around my throbbing dick, I'm a goner.

I shed the rest of my clothes and all but rip her panties away. My mind is clear enough to retrieve a condom from my pants pocket before launching onto the bed after her.

"I've waited forever," I say with a growl as I push her knees apart. "Don't make me wait any longer."

She whimpers and digs her claws into my biceps in an effort to draw me to her. I press a chaste kiss to her panting mouth before trailing wet kisses down between her breasts to her toned stomach. When I reach her pussy, she grabs on to my hair. "Can't you just make love to me already?"

I chuckle and run my tongue along her slit. "Are you sure you don't want me to taste you a little bit first?"

Her words are garbled but the moment I massage her once more with my tongue, she gives in with a moan. "Yessss."

Nipping and lapping at her perfect pussy, I devour the woman who has always held my heart in the palm of her tiny hands. I've missed her so fucking much. I can't get enough of her—I'll never get enough of her.

"I need to feel you," I breathe against her, causing her to yelp out. "From the inside."

She lets out a sound too erotic for anyone but me to ever hear the moment I push my finger into her hot, wet center. Her body grips me in that tight way I remember and I'm about to come all over her sheets.

Jesus, I've missed us.

"So tight," I praise, my finger expertly finding her nub of pleasure within. The moment I hook my finger and graze it, she jolts like a live wire.

"OH GOD!"

"That's it," I coo against her pussy, my tongue teasing her clit as I finger fuck her G-spot to oblivion. "Come all over my finger like you used to, Kady."

She squirms and thrashes until her orgasm consumes her like a demon possessing its innocent victim. It takes everything in me not to come right along with her but I want inside of her when I finally have my release.

When she eventually comes down from her high, I slip my finger from her. Her heavy breathing is my drug and it fuels me on. I tear at the condom with my teeth until I free the rubber. My dick is rock hard and eager to be inside of her again.

Kady and I are better together.

Always.

"I love you," I assure her as I tease her opening with my now sheathed cock. "Don't ever forget that. No matter where you are or what you're doing. My love never wanes."

"I know."

Her words die off into a pleasure-filled wail the moment I push every thick inch of my cock into her receptive body. Once I'm seated inside of her, I let out a groan of relief. If it were up to me, we'd live like this. She and I, connected.

"Say it, Kadydid," I murmur against her sweet lips, my voice nothing but a whisper just like she loves. "Tell me what I need to hear."

"I love you too, Yeo."

chapter eight

Kady

I sent him away back then.

   Despite his pleas. Despite his tears. Despite his near rage.

Goodbye, Yeo.

And when he damn near refused to go, I called in reinforcements. Bones and Officer Joe can be fierce when they need to be. Yeo didn't have a choice but to listen to me.

Now he's back in my arms.

Back in my heart.

No more goodbyes, Yeo.

His hot breath on my bare chest sends a thrill of excitement coursing through me and love thundering straight to my heart. With Yeo, my mind is calm and my soul is happy. I can quiet all of the awful, disgusting thoughts that tell me I'm not good enough for him and let him love me like he wants to. Usually.

But twelve years ago, a year before Grandma passed

away and I was left with a house and all the demons in it, I disconnected our link. It was the most difficult thing in my life—severing every single part of me that was tied to him. Yet, I did it. Because if I didn't, Yeo would die in my house. Unhappy. Maybe alone. Sad and confused.

And that tore me apart.

He'd isolated himself from his family and friends because of me.

It wasn't healthy and they resented me because of it.

My stupid, stubborn boy led me to believe he'd followed my orders. He did, sort of. Went off and got his education. A doctor no less. But then he came back. That wasn't the plan. Yet now, as I stroke his stick-straight inky colored hair, I'm happy. Relieved. Blessed beyond all reason.

Why won't he just forget me?

I'm too much trouble.

Depression is a part of my life. Some days, it just swallows me whole. I lie in bed for hours and hours just like Momma used to do. Hiding from the outside world. Hiding from my reflection. Replaying the negative parts of my life over and over again on some torturous loop. It's not something I simply get over. It consumes me.

Except, with Yeo, the pull is a little weaker.

And the only time I want to stay in bed is when he's naked and in it with me.

I'm too much trouble.

My skin grows cold and clammy as my troubled thoughts scamper into shadows. The present bleeds into the past. And memories of a world I try so hard to forget claw at me, dragging me under so quickly I forget to breathe and fortify myself first.

"*You're too much trouble,*" *Daddy says, his voice cold like the snow that's falling outside. My eyes flit over to the window, preferring the quiet snowfall over his mean words.*

When I don't reply, his fingertips bite into my jaw as he jerks my face to stare right at him. These days, Daddy isn't nice. In fact, I can't remember the last time he was nice. Maybe on my seventh birthday? He'd taken me down to Hobbit's Creamery and I'd gotten rainbow sherbet, my favorite, and then we'd gone to the park to play. Mommy was sick that day. I know she was sick because the night before he'd hurt her.

"Maybe I should send you to live with your grandma. What do you think about that?" he demands, his voice low and growly like Butch's. Butch almost bit my fingers the other day. Daddy looks like he might bite too.

"Can Mommy come too?" I question, hot tears forming in my eyes.

He releases his grip and stands. I rub away the soreness on my jaw as he paces my small bedroom. Just like Butch paces the fence when he's dying to get out from behind it. Sometimes I wonder if he wants to get over the fence to play with me. Other times I wonder if I look like something he could snack on.

"We were fine until..." Daddy trails off and snaps his hate-filled glare to me.

I swallow and bite on my lip to keep my chin from quivering. "Until what, Daddy?"

"It was a boy, you know. We wanted a boy."

I frown. "What was a boy?"

"The baby." His voice is sad and he hangs his head. "Your mother lost the baby last year and I...and we...I just can't..." He grabs at his hair and pulls. I'm afraid he'll rip it right from his head.

"Daddy, where did the baby go?"

He snaps his gaze to mine and for the briefest of moments, his hard features turn soft. "It died, Kadence. The baby died in your mommy's tummy."

"You want me to live with Grandma so I don't die too?"

He storms over to me and I flinch. But then he sits down on the bed beside me, burying his face in his hands. His whole body shakes as he cries. Daddy doesn't cry. Not ever. Why is he crying?

With a nervous hand, I reach over and pat his back. "It's okay, Daddy. I'm careful. Butch only tried to bite me once. I won't die."

His body tenses but he lifts his head to look over at me. "I'm sorry."

I scramble into his lap and throw my arms around his neck. Daddy hugs me to him and kisses my head. He smells like smoke and stinky beer but this hug is like the ones I remember from before he became mean.

"I love you, Daddy," I assure him.

He pats my back and kisses my head again.

Then he tickles my leg just above my knee and I giggle.

Daddy laughs too. His eyes meet mine and I don't recognize him. He has the same eyes Butch has. Like he's hungry. I shiver and he shakes away the look before tossing me on the bed and then standing to leave my bedroom.

"Go to bed, Kadence."

As I attempt to fall asleep, I can't help but smile. I fixed Daddy. When he's mad or sad, I can fix him and make him happier.

I have superpowers.

I'm dragged from my memories when I hear Yeo's murmured praise along my flesh as he kisses my breast. His dark eyes lift to find mine and he cocks up a black eyebrow in that mischievous way I love so much as he bites my nipple. I let out an appreciative gasp the moment his tongue circles the nipple to sooth away the pain.

Yeo is good at a lot of things.

But what he's best at—something nobody else can do—is keeping me out of my own damn head. He keeps me here, in the present, ensnared in his loving gaze.

Despite not having been intimate with him in so long, I recognize his body. Sure, it's changed over the years. He's stronger. Firmer. Heavier. Dark hair shades along his jawline that I don't remember from before. I sent my boy away and he came back a man. *My* man. A shiver of excitement quivers through me. Staking claim on him may seem frivolous, but to me, it feels like hope. That maybe he won't have to go away this time. Maybe I can keep him like he says… forever.

"Remember when I took your virginity?" he questions, a smirk on his handsome face. He lifts up on his knees and I'm awarded with a view of his sculpted, pale flesh, illuminated by the morning sunlight. I remember Yeo being fit, but I don't remember him being so dang muscly. Rubbing my thighs together, I reach for his chest and skitter my fingertips over one of his pectoral muscles.

"Yeah, it was perfect."

He laughs, the sounds rich and hearty. Like a hot stew filling your belly on a cold, winter night. "Kadydid," he says with a shy grin, "it was far from perfect. I came in like three seconds. Your grandma nearly busted us. Had she, I would have been grounded for life."

But that's not how I remembered it.

"I just want to feel closer to you…" I murmur, my hand sliding over the front of his jeans. He's hard. So hard. I want more than this.

"Kadydid," he groans and then his tongue spears inside of my mouth before he pulls away and frowns at me. "You can't tease me like this. I want to…I'm dying to…"

I flutter my eyelashes at him. "Grandma's not here. Maybe we could have sex."

His eyes close and his jaw clenches. If I didn't know him, I'd say he was angry with me. But Yeo is never angry with me. He's always angry for me. When everyone else is after me, it's Yeo who faces them bravely. "Kady…"

"Please have sex with me. I want to know what it feels like."

He reopens his eyes and his dark eyes are like molten lava. Hot and intense. Overwhelming. Like he wants to consume every part of me.

"Take off your shirt," he says with a growl. "I want to see your perfect tits."

I beam at him and peel away my shirt. With a flick of the latch behind me, my bra is soon gone as well. His eyes skirt over my creamy flesh as he appreciates my naked chest.

"So beautiful."

Leaning back on my bed, I work at the button on my jeans. He remains frozen as he bores his gaze into me. I unfasten my jeans and then push them down, along with my panties, to my knees. The action seems to jolt him back to life because then he takes over removing me from the last of my clothes.

His hand splays over my stomach and then his eyes meet mine. Two eyebrows pinched together as if he's in pain.

"What is it?" I question, my voice a needy whisper.

"I just..." he trails off. "Are you sure? Like are you sure, sure?"

Nodding, I give him a bright smile that seems to wash away all of his indecision because he smiles back. "Yeo, I've never been so sure about anything. When we're together, all I can think about is you. That's all I want to think about."

He tugs his shirt off and then undoes his pants. His thick cock, a cock I've sucked off many times, bounces out. I grab onto his dick and run my thumb over the tip causing him to hiss in pleasure. A bead of pre-cum wets my skin. Veins protrude from his erection, pulsating with the need to come. I've licked every single one of those veins before. His dark hair has been clipped back against his flesh making his cock seem longer and bigger than normal. Yeo may be only sixteen but he's a man in my eyes. My man.

"I want to know if I can feel those veins inside of me," I tell him, almost absently.

He grabs my wrist and grumbles. "You say things to drive me crazy on purpose, Kadydid."

I laugh. "Not on purpose. Not usually."

He nudges my knees apart and covers my body with his.

The heat from his flesh mixes with mine, creating a sticky sweat. We haven't even done anything yet. Yeo and I make fire. We ignite into a brilliant, blazing inferno whenever we're near one another. I can only imagine what sort of hellish explosion we'll make when we finally connect as sexual partners.

"I don't have a condom." His words are a whisper. I like whispers.

"I'm on the pill," I assure him. My only problem is remembering to take it.

"Thank God," he hisses as his mouth crashes to mine.

The moment his tongue is back in my mouth, I'm a squirming madwoman. My fingers rake through his hair and I wriggle beneath him, attempting to get him to slip his cock from where it rubs against my thatch of pubic hair to plunge inside of me.

"It might hurt." His words are meant to be gentle, to soothe me. But he's the one who sounds like he is aching.

"So hurt me, Yeo Anderson. Hurt me."

His hand slides between us and he grabs on to his dick. I whimper when he teases my wet opening with the tip. He's not slow or gentle like the Yeo I know. I've turned him into something hungry and needy. I love that he's lost control. I released his monster.

"I'll go fast," he promises, his words spoken just a hair before he drives forcefully into me.

Hot, white pain makes me go blind for a moment but then his lips are on mine again, bringing me back to him. Always him. I knew it would hurt. My mind threatens to retreat. Yet, I don't. I dig my fingernails into his shoulders as he thrusts into me and cry out his name over and over in a never ending chant. "Yeo Yeo Yeo Yeo!"

His breath is ragged and uneven. My composed, cool boy is out of control and I love it. I want him lost inside of me. Forever. We're untouchable now. The entire world around us can fuck off.

"Oh God, Kadence," he groans, his teeth clashing against mine. "I'm sorry. I'm going to come."

I drive my fingers into his hair and latch on. "I love you. Do it."

His eyes clench shut just moments before he lets out a noise I hope nobody on this earth but me ever gets to hear. Carnal and scorching and mine. A fiery heat explodes within me and his cock seems to double in size as he spurts his release into me.

I've never felt so loved or owned in my entire life.

So distracted.

Yeo is my entire world in this moment.

Yeo is my entire world in this moment.

"Are you hungry?" he questions, a grin playing at his lips as the past fades into the present.

My stomach, as if on cue, bubbles loudly. "Umm, no."

He kisses my belly and then gives it a little bite. "Liar. I can make cereal or cereal. Your call. My bachelor cooking skills leave something to be desired."

Running my fingers through his hair, I let out a sigh. My mind flits to what Aunt Suzy bought from Walmart. I know we have ingredients for pancakes.

"Agatha might cook for us," I tell him absently.

I close my eyes and try to envision if we have eggs in

the refrigerator. Do we have enough? Is there bacon?

Kady. Kady. Kady.

Yeo's calling for me but I'm thinking.

Thinking. Thinking. Thinking.

Six eggs. I remember that much.

Kady. Kady. Kady.

An entire bag of bacon unless Bones got into it.

Thinking. Thinking. Thinking.

Orange juice. Aunt Suzy definitely bought orange juice.

Kady. Kady. Kady.

Now I just need to tell Agatha.

Yeo. Yeo. Yeo.

Yeo deserves a home cooked breakfast.

Yeo. Yeo. Yeo.

Yeo deserves everything.

Yeo. Yeo. Yeo.

"Kady!"

Refusing to open my eyes, I let the words fall from my mouth. "Grab a shower. I'll help get Agatha started in the kitchen."

Black. Black. Black.

chapter nine

Yeo

"More bacon, pumpkin?" I lean back in my chair and rub my belly. "I shouldn't. Between you and Mom, Agatha, I swear you two will fatten me up and I'll lose all this muscle tone I worked so hard to gain."

Agatha laughs, her voice throaty as she drops two more pieces of bacon on my plate. The lotion she wears reeks of roses and mothballs and the 80s, but it's her and it's unique and I'd never change that about her. "If we fatten you up, it keeps all the girls away." At this she winks.

"As long as Kady can stay, the rest of the girls can go hang out with Dean," I say with a grin.

She tightens the ties on her cream-colored robe that she wears over one of those old lady nightgowns that's probably been around since before I was born. Her slippers are worn and used. If I didn't think it would insult her, I'd buy her a new set. But they've been around for years and are practically a part of her.

"How's your family?" she questions, pushing her bifocals down her nose to peer over them at me. "Your dad doing okay?"

I cringe at the mention of my father. Last night's dinner was a disaster and that's only a reminder. "Same. Hard and unyielding. What else is new? Did Kady tell you about it?"

Her lips press into a thin line and her brows pinch together in a worried way. "He loves you. He's just trying to protect you, you know?"

Irritation ripples through me but I nod anyway. Agatha has answers and knowledge. She's like a second mother. "I know. But in his effort to protect me, he hurts her."

"She's stronger than you think, Yeo," she assures me.

I inhale the bacon as I ponder her words. "Have you seen the inside of her thighs?"

She sits down across from me and blows on her mug of coffee. Agatha drinks it black, which has always grossed Kady and I out. "The cigarette burns?"

Tensing at her words, I nod. "Those scars weren't there last time I was with her."

Her brows scrunch together and she gives her head a slight shake. "And last time you were around her, Kenneth wasn't coming around much either. You know how he is. Pascale and him both. Like the plague in this house."

"I ran into Pascale last night," I groan, pinching the bridge of my nose. "He was packing heat."

She frowns at me.

"Pascale, believe it or not, doesn't come around much. I'm not sure why he showed up last night. Bones usually does a good job of keeping him away."

I swallow at how I'd hurt Bones's feelings last night. I've not seen him this morning. I'm not sure how long it'll take before he's ready to show his face around here again.

"Bones got my name tattooed on his nipple," I tell her with a sigh.

She chuckles. "Yes, I'm very aware of his tattoos. He loves you. We all do. You're a part of this big, crazy family, pumpkin."

"What do you think I should do?" I question. "I thought I'd come back and things would go back to the way they were. But Kady is fragile. Bones is too for that matter. My family is just as snotty toward her as the day they met her. I just want everyone to understand my love for her. All facets. Every single dirty, ugly part."

She stands and takes my plate. Agatha doesn't leave her kitchen messy for long. The sink turns on as she starts to wash. I put the leftovers away while she cleans.

"You know," she says, drying a plate, her eyes cutting over to mine. A small, mischievous smile plays on her lips. "You could call a family meeting. Show them the book you made. Tell them all about her. Maybe if they understand her, they'll show a little more compassion."

I think about the book that stays in Kady's room. A book I started for her when I was seventeen but continued to work on throughout the years—even when I was away. It helped her cope with parts of her life that needed better understanding. I'd even spoken about it a little in some of my classes whenever we'd discuss the topic. My professors were always curious but I never gave the details in a way that would betray her.

"I don't know if she'll go for it."

"So talk her into it. If she is afraid, and I need to go with you, I'd be more than happy to help explain our sweet Kady to them. You know I love you, pumpkin. I want you and her to both be happy."

I pull her to me and inhale her old lady scent. She comforts me always.

"I called a technician this morning. They'll be out later so make sure to leave the door unlocked. This house is too hot," I tell her when she releases me.

"I'll make sure to leave a note for the rest of the family. What's on the agenda for today?"

Running my fingers through my hair, I give her a weary look. "Dad's already texted early this morning. He wants to meet up at his office to look at a few buildings. When Kady comes back, I want her to come with me."

Agatha raises an eyebrow in surprise. "You want Kady to go look at buildings with your dad?"

I dip my head and give a nod. "She's a part of my world. No more hiding. He's going to have to accept that. Hell, she's going to have to accept that."

She nods. "You're right. I'll make sure to talk some sense into that girl. Run home and shower before I give you a bath in this sink, pumpkin. We'll talk later, love."

I lean forward and give her a quick peck on her cheek. "Thanks, Agatha. You're my favorite, little lady."

Her laugh is musical and warm. "You're my favorite too, Yeo."

"I like this one best, Dad. It's small but has room if I take on a partner. Overlooks the Monongahela River. Affordable. The others were too flashy and not me," I tell him as we climb into his black Range Rover, both of us waving to Rick Stanford, Dad's realtor. "I can do this on my own though. You and Mom don't have to do this."

He chuckles and flashes me one of his stubborn looks. "We're getting old. Let us do these things for you. If that's the building you want, we'll make the necessary arrangements and buy it."

"Thanks."

As he reverses the vehicle, his smile falls and he clears his throat. "Are we going to talk about last night? About Kadence?"

My blood boils at his tone. He doesn't want her in my life. Never has, never will. "What's there to say? You guys attacked her."

He stiffens and keeps his eye on the road. "We just want the best for you, Yeo. She's a weight. She drags you down. She'll always drag you down to the bottom."

I send him a scathing look. "If the bottom is where she is, the bottom is where I'll be. You can't just cut love out of your chest so easily. It doesn't work that way."

"I just don't understand how she—"

"That's right," I snap, "you don't understand. You know nothing about her. But, you know what? That's going to change. We're going to have a family sit-down and you all will have to open your minds so you can fall in love with her too."

He grumbles, obviously not convinced, and I stare

out the window watching the people walking along the sidewalks of Main Street. When I see two familiar pigtails bounce by, I reach for Dad.

"Stop the car."

"What, I—"

"Dad, stop the car right now!"

I point to a spot outside of Hank's Ice Cream and Sweets where I saw those pigtails bounce into.

"Yeo, what are we doing?"

"We're having ice cream. And you're going to meet Presley. Sweetest little nine-year-old girl you'll ever meet. Be nice," I warn.

He grunts but climbs out of the Range Rover after me. Dad looks out of place in front of the shop decked out in an expensive suit, his hard eyes roaming the store in disdain, and his sleek haircut flapping in the breeze.

We slip into the shop and I see her. Presley's in line proudly placing her order. The worker seems annoyed to be helping her which causes me to clench my fists in irritation. I'd like to grab him by his shirt to yank him over the counter and remind him he's being paid to help people. No matter what they look like.

Sneaking up behind her with Dad on my tail, I eavesdrop as the worker places her cone with mint chocolate chip ice cream in a stand beside the register. Kady would be gagging if she were here. She hates mint.

"That'll be three fifty-seven."

She digs in her small unicorn coin purse and retrieves two quarters and a penny. "Is that enough?" Her voice is small and unsure.

The man's nostrils flare as he looks down at her in annoyance. "What are you, retarded? No, it's not enough."

He barely gets the words out before I am pushing past her at the counter. I lean over and get in his face. His face smarts red with embarrassment or fear, I don't know what. "Didn't your mother ever tell you the *R* word is rude? How'd you like it if I called you pepperoni face?" I seethe and wave at his acne.

"Yeo," Dad growls from behind me.

Ignoring him, I whip out my wallet and throw a five-dollar bill onto the counter. Presley looks up at me with wide, thankful eyes. Her smile is my undoing and I calm considerably. "Keep the change, punk."

Presley giggles, carefully plucking her coins back off the counter. She puts them into her change purse and grabs my hand. I let her guide me over to a table by the windows. When she sits, I pull up an extra chair for Dad. His grey eyebrows are furled together but his lips are pressed shut into a firm line. He folds his arms against his chest and leans back in his chair as if to watch the show but not participate.

Rolling my eyes, I point at her ice cream. "Good stuff, nugget?"

She nods emphatically and licks the cone. Green ice cream gets on her nose to which she attempts to lick off.

"You look like a puppy. Only puppies can lick their noses," I tease.

I risk a glance at Dad and his anger has morphed into something else. Interest. Presley has that way about her. Draws in the entire world with her giggles and sweet disposition.

"I'm not a puppy," she pouts. "I'm a horse."

At this, I lift an eyebrow. "Why a horse? You have pigtails that look like puppy dog ears."

Her eyes narrow as she considers this. Then, she turns to my dad. "I'm Presley," she sticks out a sticky hand to shake my father's. "What's your name?"

Dad is stiff and unmoving. But when Presley's smile falls, he sits up, offering his hand. She shakes it, beaming at him. "I'm Fletcher."

"Fletcher," she tries the word out on her tongue. "Do you think I look like a puppy or a horse?" She doesn't let go of his hand. When she stands, his eyes widen for a moment. Her mouth goes to his ear as she whispers loudly. "Say horse."

"Um," he says, his voice gravelly and unsure before darting a confused glance my way. "Horse?"

She shrieks and lets go of his hand so she can point at me. "Ha! Told you so. You stink, Yeo. Fletcher is my new friend." Her lashes flutter in that innocent way that makes everyone's heart around her melt as she flits her gaze to Dad. "Aren't you?"

He's uncomfortable but he's not being rude. Progress. "Yeah, I guess. I'm your friend."

With a triumphant glint in her eyes, she continues licking her cone.

"Why are you out here alone?" I question, my eyes narrowed.

She shrugs her shoulders but gets a faraway look in her eyes. "Daddy hurt Mommy again. She couldn't get ice cream with me. I had to go alone."

A low growl in Dad's throat startles me. I flicker my eyes over to him. He now sits with his elbows on his knees, leaning toward her. Sweet, magnetic Presley.

"Did your daddy hurt you, nugget?" I ask.

Melted green ice cream runs down the back of her hand. Her lip wobbles at my question. "No."

Dad and I both sense the lie. He, surprisingly so, is the first to respond. "Who's abusing you?" The tone of his voice is protective. I'm shocked.

Her tear-filled glassy blue orbs find his. "Daddy. Always Daddy."

His chin jerks over to me and I see it. Worry and confusion and fury. He's angry for her.

"Nugget," I say softly as I tug a couple of napkins from the dispenser and hand them to her. "What can we do to help?"

Her nose scrunches up as she ponders my question. We sit for a few moments more as she licks her ice cream. Finally, she finds the nerve to answer me. "Can you make him go away?"

Dad's jaw clenches. "I could put in a call. My son's friend knows some people at the police station who might be able to help."

Her eyes brighten and she beams at Dad as if he were a hero. "Would they take him to jail? I don't like when he…" The smile on her face falls as she looks down at the table, her voice coming out in a whisper. "I don't like when he comes into my room at night."

I sense Dad is about to explode so I diffuse the situation.

"Hey, nugget? I think that cone is nothing but a mess now. Why don't you go get cleaned up in the bathroom?"

She nods as she stands. Dad lets out a grunt of surprise when she throws her sticky arms around him, hugging him tight. He doesn't hug her back but he does pat her back.

"Thank you, Fletcher," she murmurs.

His pained eyes meet mine for a brief second. "You're welcome, Presley. Go and get cleaned up."

She breaks from him and skips off to the bathroom leaving me with my father. Questions dance in his eyes. Anger pinches his brows together. Sorrow makes his rigid shoulders hunch.

"That poor girl," is all he says.

"Yep."

I can see he has a thousand questions but he keeps them locked up in his head until the time is right. Dad is known for analyzing. For fact checking. For coming to educated conclusions. It's what makes him so good at his job.

The bell chimes above the shop door and we both watch as Presley bounces off down the street and around the corner without so much as a goodbye. She's always walking to and from the ice cream shop by herself. That girl is brave and independent. I wish there was more I could do for her.

"Yeo," he says, scrubbing his palm over his face. "Please explain to me what's going on with that girl."

I scratch at my jaw before turning a raised brow at him. "Her story is sad, Dad. I'm not even sure it's my story to tell."

His mouth is opened to argue when his eyes zero in on Kadence, her long hair flowing in the breeze. She's about to pass the shop when she sees me. I wave her inside. Her smile is small and pretty but the moment she sees Dad, it falls away. Her confidence melts away and her entire body tenses.

"Uh, I was just passing by. Didn't mean to interrupt anything," she says, her voice timid.

I stand and stride over to her. Kissing her quickly on the lips, I then guide her over to the table. "Excuse the mess. We ran into Presley. She did more talking than eating. You know how that little nugget is."

She sits and her eyes skim over the green drops littering the table. "Ew, mint?"

Chuckling, I nod at her. "Want anything?"

"Rainbow sherbet, please," she says, her unsure eyes flicking over to my dad.

His body is tense as he watches her. My eyes never leave their table as I order her a bowl of rainbow sherbet. Her lips move every now and again, clearly answering his questions with those one-worded answers she's so good at. Finally, I have her sherbet in hand and stroll back over to them.

"What'd I miss?" I ask and slide her bowl over to her.

"Thank you," she says sweetly. "Um, your dad said you might have found a building. For your practice. That sounds nice."

Grinning at her, I give her a quick wink. "It was nice. If we end up getting it, Dad and I would love to show it to you. Isn't that right, Dad?"

His nod is slow but at least he's agreeing.

"I'd like that," she murmurs, scooping out a spoonful of the sherbet. "Well, as long as I don't have any lessons."

I nudge her foot under the table and send her a comforting look. Her shoulders relax a bit. A smile plays at her pink lips. I'd do anything to keep it there all day.

"We'll make it work," I assure her and take her free hand, my forearm sticking in some residue along the way. "I thought maybe we could go shopping today. Are you free? My car is at Dad's office. What do you think?"

She takes a bite of her sherbet and glances quickly over at my dad who remains silent before looking back at me. "What are you shopping for?"

"We could go furniture shopping. If I get a building, I'm going to need a desk and bookcases. Stuff like that."

Her smile is small but it's there. "Do they have kitchen tables there?"

At this, Dad leans in, his interest visible. "What do you need a kitchen table for? Do you not have one?" he questions.

Her body tenses at his words but she faces him bravely. "Someone carved their name into mine. I can't look at it without wanting to be sick."

I can tell he's about to probe her more when I cut in. "That table is old anyway. We'll find a new one."

She eats more of her sherbet while I send Dad a sad look. He's perceptive and smart as a whip. I know he's putting together pieces quicker than he lets on.

"So, Kadydid, I was just telling Dad here that I thought maybe we could have a big family dinner. Maybe one at your house. Agatha has offered to host," I tell her, a small lie. Agatha offered to help but I know she won't mind cooking for my army. "Thought maybe it would be a great way for them to get to know you better. Since I'm back for good and all."

Her eyes whip to mine, fear dwelling in them, before she flickers them over to Dad. I expect him to be all hard and imposing but he smiles. Dad actually fucking smiles.

"We'd love to see your place and meet your family, Kadence," he tells her, his voice warm and different than usual.

Her eyes widen and her plump lips part open. "Um, I don't know. Some of my family are…they are…" She jerks her gaze to mine, pleading with me. "They're bad."

I squeeze her hand. "Dad's not afraid of bad people. He deals with them all the time with his company. Isn't that right?"

Dad nods and clears his throat. "I'm curious to meet them. The bad ones as well. If they're a part of your family, then I'd like to meet them."

She swallows, fighting tears in her eyes. "Okay."

"What about Friday night?" Dad questions.

"We'll ask Agatha if she can make it happen," I tell him and give her clammy palm another comforting squeeze. "If she can buy and prepare enough food by then, we'll make it work."

"Tell Miss Agatha my Gyeong will help her cook if need be. Or, we could always have food catered. Let's make this dinner happen, though, okay Kadence?" His eyes have a sympathetic gleam to them. A gleam I remember as a child. Something fatherly and protective that always shone in his eyes. I'm about to fist pump the air over the fact that he's giving her a look he hardly even shows to my brothers.

Kadence laughs. Cute and quiet. Just like her. "Agatha would have a fit if we ordered in. You don't want to make that old lady mad," she teases. "She'll hit you over the head with a rolled-up magazine or put you to work scrubbing baseboards. It's best we let her do what she enjoys. And Agatha loves cooking. Thank you."

Dad nods at her. "I'm looking forward to it."

For the first time since I arrived back in Morgantown, things are starting to look up. Two of the most important people in my life, who have spent the better part of two decades avoiding each other, seem to finally be attempting to reach out to one another. I'm not sure how it'll all turn out but I can't help but thank God for this tiny step in the right direction.

chapter ten

Kady
Nine Years Old…

"I want to play with Yeo," I whine, my legs kicking the air beneath me as I poke at a green bean with my fork.

Grandma smiles. *"Isn't he grounded?"*

Huffing, I nod. *"He made a bad grade at school."*

"His parents are too hard on him," Mommy chimes in. Today, she's pretty. Her brown hair has been twisted up into a fancy bun. There's a dark bruise on her neck and I frown. Daddy doesn't live with us anymore, so I wonder how she got the bruise.

"Mommy, what happened to your neck?"

Grandma's grey eyebrows lift and she smiles. *"Yes, Louise, what happened to your neck?"*

Mommy's cheeks turn red and now she's the one poking at her green bean. *"Um, it was an accident."*

"Did Kevin accidentally give you that bruise on your date last night?" Grandma asks, her voice light and teasing.

Mommy seems embarrassed and Grandma seems happy. I don't understand why they're acting so weird. If Kevin is bruising my mommy like Daddy used to, I hate him.

"Who is Kevin?" I question, my bottom lip threatening to quiver.

Mommy sighs and pushes her plate away. Her eyes lift, darting over to the window. "He's my boyfriend."

"Like Yeo? Yeo is my boyfriend."

Grandma chuckles. "Yeo is your boy friend. *I think your momma's* boyfriend *is something altogether different, though."*

I frown. "I don't understand, Mommy."

Mommy turns and regards me with a shy smile. "I like him. We go on dates. He's nice to me. Sometimes we kiss." She scrunches up her nose to tease me at the last part but it makes my stomach hurt.

"Will he kiss me?" Tears well in my eyes. I want Yeo or Bones or Grandma to tell me everything is going to be okay.

"Well, it's nothing serious but eventually, who knows? I might marry him. One never knows about these things and it's certainly too early to tell but I really like Kevin. Perhaps one day he could be your stepdad."

The chair from beneath me screeches against the hard wood floors as I stand. "No."

Mommy glances at Grandma for a brief moment before regarding me with sad eyes. "Kady, not how you're thinking and—"

"I don't want him to come into my room, Mommy," I tell her bravely, my tears staying in my eyes but just barely. "I don't want another daddy."

"Honey," she tries but I cut her off.

"He already bruised you. Just like Daddy did! Daddy hurt you and then...then he hurt me..."

"It's just a hickey—"

"Louise," Grandma interjects, shooting her a stern look. My mother quiets and looks down at her lap. Then, Grandma turns toward me. "Nobody is hurting you in my house, pumpkin. Understand?"

I nod but am not convinced.

"Nobody will ever go into your room again," she tells me firmly. "Are we clear, Kadence Marshall?"

Nodding once more, I sit and go back to picking at my green beans.

"So, how did the new job go?" Grandma asks Mommy, changing the subject.

My mind travels to Daddy. Whenever I'm lonely, it's Daddy. When I'm scared, it's Daddy. When I'm upset or angry, it's Daddy.

Daddy. Daddy. Daddy.

"Kadence," Grandma says softly.

Daddy. Daddy. Daddy.

"Kadence!" Grandma and Mommy's voices fade out when I close my eyes. His eyes are in my mind, glaring at me. Accusing me. Hurting me.

No! No! No!

chapter eleven

Yeo
Twelve years old...

"**W**ould you like a slice of homemade lemon me-ringue pie?" Ruth questions, her wrinkled hands on her hips.

"Mom said dinner would be done in thirty minutes," I tell her, my eyes scanning the living room looking for Kady or Bones. "But maybe just a small piece?"

Ruth chuckles. "Have a seat then. I'll bring you some. Just don't tell your momma."

When she's gone, I'm happy to see Bones walk into the room. The kid never wears a shirt. Ever. And today, he's top-less but he's not his usual self. His shoulders are hunched and his smile is gone. I can sense he's upset.

"Hey, Bones," I say as I sit in Kady's usual place at the table. My eyes fixate on a carving near her plate. It makes me shiver.

"Hey, Kitty Muncher." His playfulness is a farce. I can see

the sadness in his eyes. Fear maybe.

"Is Kady okay?"

He scowls and crawls onto the table. Once his legs are dangling over the edge beside me, he looks down at me and fingers the fresh grooves in the wood. "Kady's never okay when Norman visits."

Anger surges through me and I glare at him. "Did he hurt her?"

He shrugs. "Not like he's done in the past. But he does scare the shit out of her."

I glance over my shoulder looking to see if Ruth heard him cuss or not. She's clanging away in the kitchen, so I'm guessing not because otherwise Bones would be sitting here with a bar of soap between his teeth.

"How do we get rid of him?" I question, anger bubbling up inside of me. "I hate him."

He pokes at my side with his bare toe in an absent-minded way. "I don't know."

We're both deep in thought—far too deep for an eleven and twelve-year-old—when Ruth arrives with two plates. One piled high with Cheetos for Bones and one with a sliver of pie for me.

"Is Kady, okay?" I ask her.

Her smile falls and she sets the plates down. She strokes the top of my head and then kisses Bones's forehead. "She will be. If you'll excuse me, I'm going to lie down. Feeling a little winded today."

When she leaves, I run my fingernail along the N carved into the table. Why does Ruth let him hurt her? Hasn't he done enough for one lifetime?

I lift my gaze and meet the stormy eyes of Bones. "We have to get rid of him."

"I could stab him," Bones offers, yanking my fork from my grip with lightning speed and pressing it to the big vein at my neck for theatrics.

I snatch it from him and shake my head. "You can't stab him or choke him or cut him or shoot him or any of those things. We have to be smart about this, Bones."

He pops one of his Cheetos into his mouth and crunches loudly while he thinks, crumbs falling down his bare chest. Ruth should make him bathe. He's dirty all over. "Right, smart. Let me think on it."

"Don't mention it to Kadence," I tell him in a low voice. "We'll just handle the problem on our own. Together we can figure something out."

"Yeah, yeah." He slides off the table and smears a cheesy finger along my cheek. "You're dirty, Kitty Muncher."

I roll my eyes and swipe my cheek with the back of my hand. "I'm serious, Bones. And don't do anything without me."

His grunt of acceptance doesn't convince me and worry floods through me. I'll have to figure something out. Quickly.

Bones doesn't exactly do anything right.

And this has to be exactly right.

chapter twelve

Yeo
Present

Her slender leg propped up on the dash as the warm wind swirls in through the sunroof of my car is enough to distract me right through a stop sign. When she squeals and points to the sign we passed, I let out a sigh and pull over on the side of the road.

"Sorry," I say, my eyes skittering over her smooth thigh to her cutoff shorts and then up her body to her face. "You distracted me."

Her shiny pink lips quirk up into a cute smile. Crimson tinges her cheeks and she bats her eyes at me in a way that stirs my cock for the umpteenth time since I've been back home. "Sorry."

I grin at her. "Don't ever change, Kadydid. You're perfect exactly how you are."

Her eyes darken and she tears her gaze from mine to stare off toward the river. "Want to go see if the water's warm yet?"

I'm hardly dressed for what I know will end up being a muddy endeavor, but she's happy and relaxed and hopeful and I'll dirty up every item of clothing I own just to keep her that way. "I thought you'd never ask."

We climb out of the car and I catch her wrist before she gets too far away. She looks over her shoulder and light dances in her eyes.

"Come here," I murmur before tugging her to me. She fits perfectly against my chest. I've missed holding her this way. A soft sigh of contentment escapes her. "I want to make you happy," I whisper.

She hugs my middle. "You already do."

Her head tilts up and I get lost in her crystal clear blue-eyed gaze. I slip my fingers into her messy hair and hold her still. My intent is to kiss her perfect lips but I hesitate just inches from her mouth. A tiny moan of need trickles from her making me smile.

"Anyone ever tell you how amazing you are?" I question, my lips brushing against her soft ones.

She chuckles as she grips my shirt. "You. Always. You're the only one." Sadness seeps into her eyes.

"They're all blind," I tell her and nuzzle my nose against hers. "Sometimes I'm greedy. I'm glad I'm the only one who sees you. If they saw just how perfect you were, they'd want to take you away from me."

Her breath hitches and tickles my lips. I press a gentle kiss to her mouth. When I go to take a breath, she parts her lips open, offering me her sweet tongue. I don't hesitate and kiss the mouth I never stop thinking about. She tastes like

k webster

ice cream and honey and cherries. Sweet and succulent and addicting. This time I'm the one groaning when I deepen our kiss, owning her tongue with mine. Her palms travel up my chest and rest on my shoulders. We eventually break from our kiss. I rest my forehead against hers, simply reveling in her lingering taste. Inhaling her unique scent that never leaves my presence.

"I'm glad they're blind then," she says, her voice full of light and love.

I give her a crooked grin. "And if they suddenly see you one day," I say with a teasing possessive growl. "Then I'll have Bones stab their eyeballs out. He'd totally do it. Am I right?"

She pulls away and laughs all the way to our secret spot. The one where we used to go to when we were teenagers. The old abandoned building by the water is still a hunk of cluttered metal and overgrown weeds. It makes it easy for us to park on a deserted stretch of road. The hole in the fence still exists so we make our way quickly over to it before any passers-by notice us.

Her tiny frame easily slips through the opening and she disappears into the thicket of trees. Now that I've bulked up some, it's harder to fit through the hole. I end up tearing my shirt on a wicked piece of fencing but thankfully it only scratches the skin instead of tearing through it. Our old path has long since grown over and I have to listen for sounds of water rushing by to lead the way. When I make it to the beachy area, she's already tearing off her shirt and revealing to the world her perfect body.

My dick lurches when she shoves her shorts down.

106

Then, with gleeful steps, she skips out into the water.

"It's warm," she says, turning back around to grin at me. Her body dips down to her shoulders. Soon, her bra and panties are thrown back to the shore.

"Don't go out too far," I warn.

She laughs. "Okay, Fletcher."

Rolling my eyes, I unbutton my dress shirt and toss it onto the beach. Her eyes never leave mine as I undress all the way down to my boxers and wade out after her.

"Fuck!" I complain. "This is not warm, Kady!"

Her giggles bounce off the water and no doubt enchant the fish swimming beneath the surface. "Oops. I lied."

Shivering, I splash toward her and then dip down to my shoulders as well. "Come here, liar."

She slips her arms around my neck and wraps her legs around my waist. I grab her hips and pull her flush against my erection that's barely contained beneath my boxers.

"I missed this," I tell her and run my nose along hers.

She sighs and leans her head back, offering me her neck. My lips find her cool flesh. Suckling her skin, I grow impossibly hard with the need to take her right here in this river like old times. When life was simpler.

Before one of the dark parts of our relationship—a time when a small mistake had a huge consequences.

Back when something great and wonderful threatened to rip us apart.

"Yeo," she purrs against my ear. "Put your cock inside of me. I need you."

My dick begs and pleads and practically tears through my boxers to chase after her perfect pussy. I grind against her, causing her to yelp out in pleasure but shake my head. "Not out here, babe. No condoms."

She pouts but doesn't press it further. The air becomes thick around us. Thick with memories of when she was just sixteen and pregnant. With our baby. We both ache from the sudden loss of it. A loss that happened without a bit of warning. A loss that ripped apart her sanity and sent my sweet girl into a tailspin of angry emotions. It wasn't until after we'd lost the baby, early on enough in the pregnancy that we were the only ones who knew about it but far along enough for it to hurt, that she told me she wasn't mentally equipped to be a mother. And she wasn't exactly keen on fathers either. One glimmer of fear—toward me of all people—shone in her eyes and I vowed I would never see that look directed at me ever again.

Simply put, Kady doesn't trust men easily.

Fathers to be exact.

And I would have been a father. To her child. The look she flashed me in that quick moment solidified the fact she'd always fear for her child like her mother feared for her. The look of fear…was I capable of doing the same atrocities her father had done to her?

Of course I would never hurt Kady or our children or anyone for that matter.

But Kady, deep down inside her heart, didn't know that.

There would always be the doubt.

And the doubt is enough to keep me pulling on a condom without fail. Every time. The doubt is what makes me the most responsible lover on the planet. I won't lose Kady. She'll always be my family. Just the two of us. That's the only way it will ever be for us.

She pulls away and regards me with a small smile. "What now, Yeo?"

Smirking at her, I tickle her ribs. "Whatever you want, Kadydid."

A thoughtful expression washes over her face as she looks past me at the moving river. Hope. It's a fleeting look, and quite frankly one I hardly ever see on her, but it's one I want to put there again and again.

"I want to stop thinking of a world without you. The punishment of all of those years was too much. My life just isn't as sweet without you. How do we make that happen?" she questions, her dark brows bunching together.

Holding her to me, I press a soft kiss to her supple lips. "It's happening now. Right now. Don't you feel it? All around us. Seeping inside of us. My love for you never went anywhere. I was just forced to lock it away. Because you asked me to. Now, I'm asking you to unlock it and free it. And toss the fucking key in the river where it belongs because I don't ever want to deny myself you ever again. We deserve to be happy, my sweet, sweet Kadence."

Our lips meet and she kisses me slowly at first. But then our kisses become urgent and needy. And if I don't get her out of this water in the next thirty seconds, I'll do something we'll regret a hundred percent later. Grabbing her ass, I lift her as I haul straight for the riverbank. Once we reach my clothes, I set her down on her back. Quickly, I shove down my boxers and dry my cock off with my shirt. I snatch out a condom, rip it open, and sheath my dick before my next breath.

As I stroke my cock through the rubber, I regard the beautiful woman stretched out on the banks. Her dark hair is halfway wet, tangled and messy as fuck, but I want it in my grasp. I want her screaming my name as I drive into her over and over without a care of anyone seeing us.

"Spread your legs apart and let me see you," I instruct as I move to stand right beside her.

That pretty crimson flush blankets her creamy skin in a way that has me wanting to say the naughtiest things I can think of to keep it there always.

"Yeo," she whimpers, her fingers tickling over her nipples, hardening them with her touch. "Don't make me wait, crazy man."

I lift an eyebrow at her and grin. "What do you want, greedy girl?"

"You. Inside me. Now." Her voice is husky and has a slight growl to it.

Dropping to my knees, I grab onto her thighs and open her up to me. Her pussy beckons me like always. Water droplets dance down past the little strip of dark hair and past her swollen lips. Speaking of lips, I lick my own and flash her a hungry stare.

"No…" she groans. "Not that. Not now. I need you."

Giving up on my quest to eat her out until she screams, alerting anyone within hearing distance of our deviant ways, I climb on top of her. She lets out a gasp when our flesh connects. I grip my throbbing dick and tease her opening with the tip.

"You want me to fuck you, Kadydid?"

Her lips twitch with amusement. "I want you to make

love to me."

I could never deny her anything she asks. Certainly not that. I rest my palm beside her face as I push my cock into her. She clutches onto my shoulders, her nails practically puncturing the skin, and she uses her heels to force me in all of the way. But I like teasing her and resist driving all of the way into her like she wants me to. When she pouts, something that makes my cock seem to grow incredibly harder, I give this beautiful woman her wish.

"AHHH!" she moans as I slam into her, the sound of our slick skin slapping its own little song on the riverbank.

I crash my mouth to hers, our teeth knocking together, as I thrust into her. Over and over. Harder and harder. I kiss her hard and soft and long and sweet. Never enough with Kadence. I'm always left yearning for more of her. I crave every single facet, every broken piece of her. I want them all collected and locked away in my heart where they belong.

She's moaning and squirming but she's not coming. I'm about to orgasm any second now—years and years of not being with her has done that to me and will take several times to break. Sneaking a hand between us, I massage her clit the way she loves while never losing stride between us.

"Come for me, Kadydid," I grunt against her lips. "Show me how good I make you feel."

Her whimpers become ragged breaths of need as she gives in to her carnal urge to climax. A ripple courses through her body before she cries out my name, shuddering with pleasure afterward. It's enough to have me losing control. The desire to close my eyes is strong but the need to see her bright blue eyes shimmering with love and pleasure is stronger.

"Yessss," I breathe against her mouth as I empty my seed into the thin barrier separating us. "So perfect."

My cock stops throbbing so intensely, and I settle onto my elbows. Her lips are parted and swollen, a pink hue forming around them from the shadow of hair that's barely begun to stubble my face.

"Life's just easier with you," she murmurs, her eyes full of light and love.

"It's time to relax, beautiful, and let me take care of you like I was born to do. Let's get home and showered. I want to take you to dinner tonight. Just us."

The light darkens and her lips fall into a pout. "What if I ruin dinner? Again?"

I run my fingers through the hair near her temples and massage the side of her head with my thumbs. "You didn't ruin anything. When are you going to get it through your thick skull that I don't care about anyone else? I don't care about what they think or what they say. All I care about is you. Learn it. Memorize it. Don't fucking forget it, Kadydid."

Her mouth parts to say something else in argument, but I press my lips to hers. My mouth whispers my words into hers. "Don't fucking forget it."

"Are we going to your house for dinner?" she questions as I guide her down the street toward my house.

"Yep," I tell her, squeezing her hand. "But don't worry. Mom went out with Dad, so it'll be just us. Don't stress."

She stops and shakes her head. "You're going to cook?"

Laughing, I point at the pizza man already sitting in my driveway. "Nope. Dominoes is cooking tonight."

Her laughter is sweet and addicting as she runs toward my house. The summer dress she's wearing is short and flies up every time she kicks up her legs, revealing to me her sexy pink panties. We had sex again after our shower on her bed and I'm already dying to be inside of her again.

"Wait up," I call out as I chase after her.

When I reach her, I wrap my arms around her waist and pull her to me. She screams—loud and uncaring of who will hear—until I put her back on her feet.

I release her and she wanders into my yard straight for Mom's rose bush by the front porch. She bends over and once again shows her pretty panties to me. And the fucking delivery guy.

"How much?" I snap, making him jerk his gaze away from my girlfriend's ass back to mine.

"Uh, thirty-seven fifty-three," he stammers. I can tell his eyes want to wander back over to her but I hold his gaze.

When I pay him and take the food, I make sure to block his view as he leaves. Once he's safely gone, I nod with my chin up to the house. "Let me feed you, beautiful."

Her cheeks turn rosy and her bright blues twinkle with delight. This is the Kady I've loved for so long. The Kady that's been hiding since I left.

I missed her so fucking much.

"What are you going to feed me?" she teases, her eyes darkening with lust.

She missed me so fucking much too.

"Well," I say as we climb the steps and head inside, "I'm going to feed you actual food because you're wasting away."

At this she makes a harrumph.

"But then..." I set the food down on the counter and turn to her with a wicked grin. "Then I'm going to feed you your dessert. Every thick, long, delicious inch of it."

She giggles, oh-so fucking cute, and pokes me in the stomach. "Dessert is supposed to be sweet, not salty."

"I'm Korean. We don't like sweet desserts," I argue, although my argument is weak considering she's known me since I was ten years old and knows that I certainly have a sweet tooth that matches hers.

"I forgot...you like rice cakes," she says, pretending to gag.

"I like *you*. You're pretty sweet."

She throws her arms around my neck and kisses me softly. "Bones would beg to differ."

I slip my hands up under her dress, gripping her ass through her panties and squeeze her to me. "Bones isn't here, therefore his argument is invalid."

"It's a good thing. He'd eat all of our pizza."

"I didn't order Cheetos flavored anything, so I think we're safe."

She pulls away from me and smiles before lifting the lid. "Our favorite," she gushes.

I grab a couple of plates from the cabinet and let her serve up our pepperoni pizza with extra mushrooms.

"What are we drinking?" I question as I saunter to the refrigerator.

She shrugs. "Got any beer?"

I pull out a cold bottle of white wine. "Nope, but we have this."

Once we're settled at the table, she tells me what her plans are for the rest of the week. Lessons on several of the days. I plan to cut out during those times and look at a few more properties. Maybe also call my good buddy Kush Pawan. If I plan on making this practice actually work and also on giving Kady the attention she needs, then I'm going to need someone like Dr. Pawan dedicated to the cause. His father wants him back in Mumbai, but Kush is a rebel like me. Together we could actually make this work.

"I think you're trying to get me drunk," I tell her after the second bottle of wine.

She pulls my empty glass away and sets it on the coffee table. I groan when she straddles me. Her lips quirk up into a devious grin that has me wanting to rip her panties off before her next breath. "Maybe I like it when you get drunk." Her voice is a soft purr that hardens my cock between us.

"What's your play, Kadydid?"

She shrugs and dips down to capture my lips with hers. My fingers dig into her hips to grind her against me while we kiss. "I don't have a play."

"Is this about Bones? Did he tell you to get me drunk?" I lean back and search her eyes for deception.

A flicker.

One tiny flicker and I know.

"This is about Bones."

Her lip trembles and my finger twitches to stop it. When she doesn't say anything, I do reach up and press the pad of my fingertip to her soft, swollen lip. She grabs my wrist with her eyes on mine, and slips her mouth around my finger. A groan rumbles through me as she sucks on it like she would my cock.

Needy. Greedy. Quickly. All eyes on me. Desire painting her every feature.

"Kady..."

She slides her lips from my finger and frowns. "I was trying to soften you up. He wants to talk to you. Hates how things were left between you two. You're easier to talk to when you've been drinking."

Grabbing her hips, I gently push her onto the sofa beside me. "I become *too* easy to talk to. You know what happens when he...he..." I let out a frustrated sigh. "Everything becomes way too fucking confusing." Running my palm across the back of my neck, I attempt to massage away some of the stress knotting up the muscles there. "I can't do this with him. I'm here with you and I don't want to jeopardize that."

When she remains quiet, playing with the hem of her dress, but not making eye contact with me, I begin to sense her sadness through my tipsy haze. Bones is her best friend. If he hurts, she hurts. If she hurts, I hurt.

"Kady," I say with a groan, clutching on to her hand and pulling it to my mouth to kiss it. "Last time Bones and I 'talked,' it ended with him sucking my dick."

My gaze finds hers to gauge her reaction. Her cheeks turn pink and she smiles. "It makes him happy to make you happy. You know that."

"But I want to make *you* happy. Yes, I love him…in a different type of way. I'm not denying that at all," I say, my voice growing husky with emotion. "But not how I love you. You're asking me to lead him on. This gets worse and worse every year, babe. He falls deeper and deeper. For me, I question my morality. It's not healthy. I'm here now and we're striving for a healthy relationship. One that doesn't involve Bones in our bed when the mood strikes."

Her lip wobbles and she nods. "I know…but…" Her breath comes out in a ragged sigh. "Give him one more night of intimacy. He'll need closure, Yeo. Please," she chokes out, "you have no idea how much he needs this for his survival."

Clenching my jaw, I try desperately to keep the words in my mouth. Words that will sting. Words that will flay my beautiful Kadence Marshall. But the words are too strong, too violent, too demanding in their need to be said. "For us to move on, his survival *isn't* necessary. In fact, it's a burden."

As soon as the words leave my mouth, I want to gather them frantically from the air and shove them back inside until I choke to death on them. Fuck. Fuck. Fuck.

She shuts down. Just like I motherfucking knew she would.

I just broke her heart.

And I broke mine in the process.

chapter thirteen

Yeo
Two years ago...

"I need to see her!" I roar, my voice a storm of fury and anger. "Fucking find her and bring her to me!"

Bones laughs—fucking laughs at me—as he tips the bottle of tequila back, drinking straight from the bottle. Once he swallows with a wince, he regards me with heated eyes. "She's not coming. You know this."

"BECAUSE YOU'RE HIDING HER FROM ME!"

I sway and curse myself for getting drunk with him in the first place. I'm home for a week before I have to get back to Connecticut. Like always, I came over in hopes of getting her to talk to me. And like usual, she hid. It pisses me off something fierce.

"Calm down, Yeo. Let's talk."

He takes a step toward me and I hold up a palm. "Talking with you ends badly."

His eyes light up and he smirks. "I didn't hear you

complaining last time."

"It's not right," I seethe through clenched teeth.

He saunters straight over to me and clutches my jaw in his brutal grip. His eyes are dark pools of blue as he glares at me. "It doesn't feel wrong, Kitty Muncher."

At this, I can't help but smile. And he makes his move. His palm slides down the front of my jeans so he can grip my hardening cock through the material. I close my eyes and think of her. Always her. It isn't fair to Bones but I can't help it.

"Bones…" My attempt at an argument is weak and trails off as he works me roughly, making my dick angry and eager for him. "We can't…"

He laughs. "Actually, we can. We can do whatever the fuck we want. Do you see anyone stopping us? Hell, we're in Agatha's kitchen and she's not telling us no. This isn't like when we were kids, Yeo. Nobody dictates what we do. Just us. Now shut the fuck up and let me make things better."

My jeans loosen as he undoes the top button. I let out a rush of breath when the sound of my zipper echoes in the kitchen. As soon as my pants are loose, his hand dives inside of my boxers to grab my cock.

Stars.

Motherfucking stars.

I've whacked off more times than I can count between my visits back to Morgantown. I haven't strayed from Kady's world. The only time I come, not by my own hand, is when Bones steps in and releases the sexual tension. It's wrong and sick but I don't think I could have survived this long without it. She hides from me. She freezes my heart with her indifference. And yet…I still keep coming back for more. Bones gives me what Kady refuses to. It's fucked up beyond all reason, but I can't stop.

My jeans fall to my ankles, and I groan when he shoves my boxers down along with them. I refuse to open my eyes. I can't look at him. It fucks with my head if I do. I'm lost in thought when his warm mouth slides over the tip of my cock. A hiss rushes from me and I spear my fingers into his long hair. I grip him hard but let him dictate the speed at which he sucks me off.

"Oh, God…"

His expert hands are stroking my cock and fondling my balls as he takes me deep in his throat. My mind is on her. Kady. Kady. Kady. I miss her. Jesus Christ, how I miss her.

"Kady," I whisper. She loves it when I whisper. "Come back to me."

But she doesn't. Bones keeps sucking my cock like he was born to do so. I try not to drown in my self-loathing. How I pretend it's Kady who's about to make me come. Always Kady.

"This isn't right." Reality attempts to claw me from the delicious way my balls tighten with the need to come. Bones is a motherfucking pro at sucking cock.

He doesn't respond but instead takes me so deep, his teeth are at the base of my dick. His throat seems to swallow me. That's when I lose all control. My release tears through me like a lion ripping open the gut of a zebra. The groans and pleasure-filled grunts pour from me like a symphony of satisfaction and desire.

"Fuck!" I roar, my cock gushing into him like Niagara

Falls. "Fuck!"

I'm pissed and drunk and goddamn stupid.

His mouth slides from my cock. I sneak a peek. I can't help it. Shimmering blue eyes look up at me as slobber drips from his chin. Fucking breathtaking sight. My thumb strokes his temple and I tell him with my eyes what my voice cannot.

Not one to get sentimental, he wipes the drool away with the back of his hand and tucks me back into my boxers. He stands and saunters off to the cabinet while I pull my jeans back up and right myself.

"Want some Cheetos, Kitty Muncher?" he questions, his back to me.

My heart threatens to rip from my chest. This is all so fucked up. So fucked up. "Bones, listen…"

He turns around and grins crookedly at me. "You're not gay, I know."

I shake my head and rake my fingers through my hair. "You know that's not what I mean. I don't give a damn about that shit. What I mean is," I say with a grumble and sigh, "I'm sorry."

His gaze drops to the floor for a moment. When he speaks, his eyes don't meet mine. "Kady misses you so fucking much."

A lump forms in my throat. "I miss her too."

"She's a dumbass for avoiding you."

"She has her reasons," I argue.

"They're stupid, fucked-up reasons."

I swallow and go to him. My arms wrap around his bony frame so I can hug him to me. Bones isn't affectionate but he lets me this time. We stand there together, our hearts thundering against the other for what seems like forever.

Then Agatha is here.

Soothing my broken heart with words of encouragement.

"She'll come back to you eventually, pumpkin."

I know this.

Deep down, I do.

But it doesn't hurt any less.

"I hope so."

chapter fourteen

Yeo
Present

She left.

Just up and left me mid-conversation.

Granted, I said some hurtful shit that I didn't mean and wish I could take back.

But I can't and she left.

"Fuck," I grunt, gripping at my hair so it sticks straight up. "Fuccccck."

The front door creaks open and my heart soars. She came back. My Kady is strong and she came back. Yet, as soon as the person rounds the corner, I see that it's not her.

"Where's Kady?" Mom asks as she tosses her purse on the table. Dad follows her in and takes his seat in his recliner.

"We had an argument. I said something I shouldn't have," I admit with a frustrated sigh.

Dad's ears seem to perk up and he leans forward in his

chair, resting his elbows on his knees. "What'd you say?"

I swallow and send an uneasy glance to my mother. She doesn't know everything but she knows enough. And after the ice cream shop run in with Kady, Dad is starting to piece it together. They both have always assumed she's just a loon. Only I know why she behaves the way she does.

"I told her Bones's survival wasn't necessary. That we'd be better off without him right in the middle of our relationship."

Mom's eyes widen. "That wasn't very nice, Yeo."

"I know," I growl. "But she..." I trail off and stand. "Whatever. It doesn't matter. I'm going to patch things up with the both of them."

Dad frowns and he regards me with a look I don't recognize. Worry. He's worried about me. Hell, I'm worried about me. I thought with how well I knew Kady...with all of the education I received...with all the rotations in the psych ward that I'd have a grip on all of this when I came back.

But I'm just as lost.

Just as frustrated.

Just as confused.

Why can't I fix everything?

"We're still on for that dinner on Friday?" Dad questions, his voice soft and gentle. It's unusual coming from him and it makes me want to crawl into his lap like I used to do when I was a small boy.

"Yeah, Kady may bail. In fact, I know she'll bail. I'm not sure who I can get to come but Agatha is pretty good about keeping her promises to me. She'll cook. But please,"

I say, looking at each of them. "Please tell Dean and Barc and everyone that they need to come over prepared to listen. I won't have them burning her at the proverbial stake like some witch. Promise me everyone will be prepared to listen. Kady is a part of me. I'm going to marry her. She'll be a part of this family. And if you all love me, you're going to have to love her too."

Mom's eyes well with tears and she hurries over to hug me. "Of course."

My gaze flits over to Dad and he gives me a nod.

"Thanks, guys. Seven is good. Text me who all is coming and I'll have Agatha make sure to prepare enough food," I tell them as I head to the door.

The walk to Kady's is quiet on this warm night. I doubt she'll be there. She wants me to talk to Bones, so I will. I'll end the sort of weird relationship we had going on while she was avoiding me all those years. He'll be devastated—I know this—but true to Bones, he'll try and hide it with jokes and insults. It kills me to have to do this. But I need Kady one hundred percent.

As I approach the house, I can hear sad, melodic piano notes filtering out into the night from the open window in the living room. Sometimes Bones's and Kady's music is hauntingly similar. Hers tends to be sadder while his is more angst ridden. It's hard to believe they both learned from Kady's grandma Ruth because they have such different styles. Tonight, even though the music is sad, I know it's Bones. There's a certain sharpness to the way he hits the keys. A certain amount of abuse the innocent ivory keys endure at his hands.

With a sigh, I climb up the steps and enter the house. It's dark inside so I follow the sound of the music. The only thing lighting up the living room is the cherry of Bones's joint. He's high. Great.

"Bones."

His music slows but he doesn't stop. If anything, his playing becomes louder. Harsher. Angrier. Walking over to him, I place my hands on his shoulders and knead the muscles. He attempts to shake me off, but I'm stronger and bigger and win. Eventually his music slows again until it stops altogether. His shoulders hunch and he lets out a sigh.

"You're fucked up, Kitty Muncher."

"I know this."

He takes another hit but doesn't offer to share. I never partake but I find it odd he isn't trying to push it on me as usual.

"I didn't mean what I said to her. You know that. I was just angry and frustrated."

"You wish I weren't here. That it was just you and Kady without me sandwiched in between you two."

Do I wish that?

How would I feel if I never spoke to Bones again?

Sick. Devastated. Broken.

"Of course I don't wish that. You've always been a part of her. You're my best friend, Bones. I don't wish that shit and you know it. I'm just trying to figure out a way to spend more time with her. She's always running…and you're not. I'm sorry, okay?"

He shakes away my touch and stands. When he goes to stalk off, I snatch his bicep. In the dark, I can't make out his expression, but I do feel his rage. It rumbles and cuts through the blackness like a gnarly knife.

"She already told me what she wanted. That you were going to come here and what, Yeo? Give me a goodbye fuck and then pretend I don't exist? Fuck you, Yeo. FUCK YOU!"

He never calls me by my name. I've royally messed shit up. His arm jerks from my grip and he storms upstairs. I'm hot on his heels. No words are coming from my lips. Every apology, every regret, every promise—they all scratch to escape but I grit my teeth to keep them contained.

His bedroom door slams, but before he can lock it, I'm shoving my way through. He throws his shirt at my face and I swat it away. When I hear the springs creak on his bed, I know he's attempting to avoid me by going to sleep. Tearing off my shirt and kicking off my shoes, I climb in after him.

The bedroom is pitch black because he covers his windows with blackout curtains. But I don't need to see him to know what he's feeling. His hurt hangs thickly in the air. Sidling up behind him, I wrap my arm around his middle and pull his back to my chest. He's tense as fuck but doesn't push me away.

Progress...

I can repair this between us.

"I'm sorry, Bones." I whisper against the back of his head. His scent is familiar—a scent I love.

"Words, Kitty Muncher. Motherfucking words."

A growl escapes me and I nip at his bare shoulder. I know what he wants. And therein lies the dilemma. When Kady disappears and abandons me and forces me on Bones,

127

I don't know what's right or wrong. Truth is, Bones is my best friend. I love him. It's unhealthy and wrong, but I do.

I bite him again, this time harder, like I know he likes. He grunts which makes my cock harden. Licking away the sting of my bite, my fingers creep to the nipple I know has my name inked on it. He did that for *me*.

I can do this for *him*.

With a delicate touch that is a stark contrast to the way I nibble at his shoulder, I run circles around his nipple until he's panting.

"Bones," I whisper against his flesh. Bones likes whispers, too. "Why do you make my life so fucking hard?"

His chuckle is throaty but at least he's laughing. "That's why you like me, Kitty Muncher. Besides," he says, his voice growing serious, "I've never left you. So don't fucking leave me. Not now, not ever. We're in this together. Do you remember the summer you turned fifteen? When Kady found those family pictures?"

My eyes close and I remember with him.

"HE DID WHAT?" I roar, my chest heaving with fury.

"He came over, destroyed her fucking room, and then left her a note detailing every explicit thing he wished he could do to her. It was fucked up, Kitty Muncher. Said he'd peel her clothes from her body and—"

"STOP!"

"I'm just relaying what happened—"

"Bones, stop," I beg. "I can't hear it. I don't want to know."

His brows furrow together as he regards me. Then, he steps forward and squeezes my bicep, pulling me to him. He hisses out his words into my ear. "I have to endure this shit twenty-four-seven with her. Norman is a fucking psycho prick. Why the fuck won't he just leave her alone? Why?"

Emotion chokes me and I shrug my shoulders. I'm surprised when Bones hugs me. And I hug him back.

"What do I do?" I ask him. "How do I fix this? Jesus, I need to fix this."

His body is tense. "If I knew, man, I'd be the motherfucking task force captain leading the goddamned brigade. But I don't know. Fuck, I don't know." He rakes his fingers through his hair and then pulls as if he might be able to tug the answers right from his brain.

"What does Officer Joe think about Norman showing up here?"

"He's all business as usual. Says he'll keep an eye out. To keep Kady away from bullshit that upsets her. Norman seems to feed off her discomfort. Like he has a sixth sense and knows when she's at her weakest. Just shows the fuck up and rocks our entire world in the process."

"What happened?"

"Before that fuckface pervert showed up, Kady had been cleaning out a closet like Grandma Ruth had asked her to. She came across a box from her room at the old house. The house before you and me and Grandma Ruth and everybody fucking else. Apparently finding pictures of your daddy and dead mommy smiling when times were happier is a buzzkill. I'm surprised Kenneth didn't show up and slit her wrists for her. Fucking asshole."

Rage blooms in my chest at the very idea of that razorblade carrying motherfucker anywhere near my Kady. "Where's the box?"

I'm already storming up the stairs with Bones hot on my heels. When I make it to her bedroom, I see the box sitting right there on the bed, contents strewn out. The pictures in question have dried tear drops on them that have smeared the ink. Without a word, I start collecting all of the items and shoving them back into the box. Bones doesn't help me. Instead, he sits on top of her dresser and pulls the cap from one of the lipsticks her grandma only recently let her start wearing. With a steady hand, he writes a note on the mirror of her dresser.

FUCK NORMAN.

Once I have the lid on the box, I prop it on my hip and make my way over to him. He hands over the lipstick and I add a note of my own.

I'll protect you from him, Kadydid. Always.

Bones nods when I hand the lipstick back to him. He then scrawls beneath our notes.

Love, Bones and Kitty Muncher—your best friends.

I flash him a smile before stalking out of the house with her box of upsetting memories. I'll keep it at my house until, one day, she can handle seeing them. I don't know if she'll ever be able to see them. But I do vow to protect her heart. Always.

"Has Norman come by since I've been back?" I question,

my hot breath tickling the flesh on his neck.

"Nope. Neither has Kenneth. Pascale showed up the other night but I haven't seen him since."

I let out a breath of relief. "Good. We can fix this again, Bones. You and I. We did it once before. Let's do what needs to be done for our girl."

"You got it, Kitty Muncher," he says, a smile in his voice.

I'm content with nibbling and sucking on his flesh while I play with his nipple but Bones has other plans. His hand cups my dick through my jeans causing me to groan with pleasure.

"Bones," I growl in warning.

He laughs—motherfucking laughs—at me per usual. "Take your pants off, Yeo."

When I close my eyes and still, he takes it as my refusal. But Bones doesn't take no for an answer. Ever. He rolls over to face me and pushes me onto my back. His deft fingers make quick work of unfastening my pants. Before I can articulate a reason why we shouldn't, he's already stripped me bare. His hand closes around my rigid bare cock and he strokes me forcefully. Bright stars light his dark room.

"Condoms. Lube. Bedside drawer," he barks.

I can hear him shedding his clothes.

I'm frozen though.

Love and my moral compass duel in the dark night. Love is more fierce and unstoppable and fucking crazy. Love always wins. That moral compass never stood a chance.

"On your knees," I instruct him as I yank the drawer open. Once I've fumbled my way in the dark and have sheathed my cock with a condom, I squirt a healthy amount of lubricant on my finger. "When's the last time you took it in the ass?"

He laughs. "When's the last time you took me in the ass?"

Christmas. The last time was Christmas. He's going to need to work up to it again.

"Relax and give me that ass," I growl.

Our ragged breaths create a wicked symphony in the darkness. Two hellish demons up to no good while our angel plays hide-and-seek with us.

I stroke his ass reverently before locating his tight, puckered hole. When I slowly push into his ass, he lets out a pleasure-filled moan.

"Feel okay, Bones?"

"Fuck yes," he grunts. "Say my name again."

So many times I've fucked with both our heads by calling him Kady because I'd missed her so fucking much. It was wrong. I was wrong.

"Bones," I murmur as I pump my finger in and out of him. With each movement, he tightens around my digit. My cock won't last long inside of him. It never does.

"More," he says, his voice needy.

I pour more lube down the crack of his ass. Then, I gently begin pushing another finger into him.

"Jesus! Fuck!"

"Too much?" I question, my movements slowing.

"No...not enough. I need more, Yeo."

I smile in the dark. Yeo. I like when he says my name too. Obeying this unusual character, I work to add another finger. In and out. Stretching and filling. This isn't our first go-around at sex like this, so before long, his ass is primed and ready. Ready for me to fuck him into tomorrow.

"Will this be the last time?" he questions, his breaths uneven.

I pull my fingers from inside of him and wipe them on the sheet. "I don't know," I tell him honestly. "I hope not."

"Do it," he urges. "Do it now."

"Flat on your belly. You're going to need to muffle your screams in the mattress," I tell him with a growl.

He obeys and I waste no time teasing his hole with the tip of my lubed cock. I have to hold it firmly in place as I push into him. The resistance is strong at first but soon, I make it past the tight ring of muscle. His scream is other-worldly and muted and mine.

"Tell me to stop…"

"Don't stop."

And so I don't.

In the dark room, my bliss becomes white as I drive slowly into his taut body. It's just as fucking satisfying as the last time. With Bones and I, it's not just sex. It's two best friends uniting in a way not many friends do. It's joining and fusing, our souls linking. It's love.

"Oh God," I whisper. Bones, like Kady, loves it when I whisper. "You're perfect."

"Say my name."

"Bones. I'm fucking inside of you, Bones. Do you hear me?" I hiss, my thrusts picking up pace. Every movement is torture on my cock and I'm blinded by lust and need. The urge to fuck him until it hurts is strong but I don't fuck him.

I make love to him.

Covering him with my body, my sweaty chest against his back, I suckle and nip at his neck as I move inside him. My arms slip beneath him and I hug him to me. Each thrust is an apology. A kiss. A hug. Another way to tell him I love him too. Bones doesn't do words...he needs actions. He needs to feel the love.

His body tenses, which makes his ass clench around my cock. When his body begins to quake as he hisses, I know he's found his release. It's all I need to push me over the edge as well. With my lips against his shoulder, I whisper, "I love you, Bones."

He's silent as I climax. My cock throbs with delicious pleasure inside of him. The bright whites fade to grey and eventually muted black as I relax on top of him.

Neither one of us moves. We're linked, and at the moment, it feels right.

"You're such a girl, Kitty Muncher," he teases, his voice hoarse from screaming with pleasure.

"I learned it from watching you," I bite back with a smile.

We both chuckle. When it grows silent again, I slip my softening cock from him and find his jaw so I can direct his face to mine. I kiss him hard, right on the mouth.

"I love you," I remind him, my voice not a whisper. Bones likes roars sometimes.

"Say my name."

"Bones."

"You hungry?"

"Not hungry for Cheetos if that's what you're asking."

He slides off the bed and away from me. I lie there, inhaling his lingering scent. My mind is fractured. Severed in two. There's no right answer here. Only what feels right.

"Hey, Kitty Muncher?" he calls out from the bathroom doorway.

A light brightens the dark space and I wince. "Yeah?"

"Love you too, fucker."

At that, he slams the door. The shower turns on and I can't help but smile up at the ceiling.

Sometimes love is fucking ridiculous.

chapter fifteen

Kady

It's been several days since Bones and Yeo patched things up. They've never been ones to fight or hold a grudge so when the air was bad between them, we all suffered. Now that they're back to being the best of friends, Yeo and I have settled into a lovely routine.

During the day, I hold my piano lessons in my nice cool house. *Thank you, Yeo.* He works on finding a place for his private practice while I'm busy with my piano students. Then, he comes by after and we spend the rest of the evening together. Well, aside from last night. Last night he'd wanted me to go to the store to pick up the food for tonight, but I just couldn't. I sent Agatha with him. They came home with enough food to feed an army. I'd worried about how much she'd spent but was informed Yeo bought all of it.

Food for the dinner with his family.

Smokes for Bones.

Another unnecessary but cute dress for me.

Cheetos for Bones.

A new scarf for Aunt Suzy.

Coloring books for Presley.

New Sharpies for Agatha.

A toy for Whiskers.

Badass aviator shades I'm jealous of for Officer Joe.

And a journal for me.

He shouldn't have gotten all of that stuff for me and my family. It probably cost a fortune but he'd been beaming from ear to ear afterward. That's just Yeo. He loves doing for others.

"Are you going to sit with me while I tell them?" he questions from the bathroom doorway, dragging me from my thoughts.

I run the lipstick over my lips and put the cap back on before shrugging my shoulders. "I don't know."

He's leaned up against the doorframe, his muscles stretching the fabric of his ice blue button up shirt. A silky, thin tie hangs from his neck and his black hair is sculpted in such a way that it sticks up in every which direction but looks really damn cool. His black slacks hug his toned legs perfectly. My Yeo looks so good, I want to rip off all of his handsome clothes and let him take me right on the bathroom sink.

But, alas, his family will be here soon.

"Does Agatha need me to do anything? The house smells fucking delicious. Her lasagna is the best."

I smooth out my black and white Aztec patterned dress and try to calm my jittery nerves. "She's already done what she can. All we need now are the people."

He flashes me a proud grin. A grin that says he loves me and thinks I'm beautiful. A grin that believes I'll make it through this dinner alive and well. Sadly, I'm going to steal his smile.

Like always.

"Where's your book?" he asks as he reaches for my hand.

I let him clasp mine. He pulls me from the bathroom and into my room.

"In the top drawer. Are you sure this is a good idea?" I'm feeling sick to my stomach and dizzy. "What if they laugh? I don't know if I can handle this."

He stops and cups my face with both of his hands. His dark gaze narrows at me as his jaw clenches. "If they laugh, I will shove them out of this house and they'll miss Agatha's icebox strawberry pie. They'll behave just for that." At this, he winks.

I smile and close my eyes. "But what if…"

He silences me by pressing his lips to mine. Warm and soft. Inviting. Wet and parting to kiss me deeper. I accept him and meet his tongue with mine. His taste is minty, and I want to spend the entire night licking his perfect mouth, not explaining myself to his snooty family.

His hands roam down to my ass and he lifts my dress. Heat blossoms over my flesh. I'd give anything to cancel dinner, let Yeo fuck me right against my dresser, and eat lasagna in bed.

He pulls me to him, his erection poking into my belly. I bet if I begged sweetly, he'd cancel dinner in a flash.

But I can't do that.

He wants to come out in the open. To allow me a voice to explain myself. To make them see why I am the way I am. As much as I loathe the idea of being exposed for all to see, I know it's the only option. The only way for us to move forward in our relationship. We're going to need his family's support.

"Kadydid," he murmurs against my lips, "I'm going to look like a perv greeting my parents with a boner."

I chuckle and grab him through his slacks. "I could take care of that real quick—"

He groans when the doorbell rings. "Later, beautiful. We'll continue this later."

When he pulls away, the fear consumes me as reality sets in. What if their hate overshadows their understanding? What if they encourage him to leave me? What if they make fun of me?

Blackness swarms in around me. Angry and unsettling. I reach up and grab at my hair in frustration.

Kady. Kady. Kady.

He's calling for me, but I'm drowning. His whispers are drowned out by the goddamned roars.

Bad girl. Bad girl. Bad girl.

Norman's hateful words are on the forefront of my mind, reminding me of who I really am.

Kady. Kady. Kady.

Tears well in my eyes and I worry about my freshly applied makeup.

What a fucking mess you are, Kady. A dirty, bad little girl. You look just like your whore mother.

I'm fighting the hell storm in my head when two warm

139

arms wrap tightly around me. Yeo knows I love it when he whispers. But, this time, he doesn't whisper.

He roars.

KADY! KADY! KADY!

His deep voice rumbles right through me and cuts through the haze of my mind as if he's wielding a knife. I blink and see his loving brown eyes focused on me. Always me. His lips moving—calling for me. Always me.

No whispers, only roars.

"KADY!" his voice roars like a bear warning off predators away from his young. "KADY!"

Snap.

Gone.

Just like that.

This is why I need my Yeo.

He's got this way about him.

"We better answer the door," I murmur.

Relief washes over him and he kisses me chastely on the lips as the doorbell rings again. "Thank you for coming back, Kadydid," he whispers back.

I like it when he whispers.

"Dinner was lovely," Gyeong says with a smile. "You'll have to pass that on to…"

"Agatha. Her name is Agatha." My words are clipped and harsh. I've attempted to be social but I'm about to have a panic attack with all of them in my space.

"I'm sorry she couldn't join us," she says, her smile

faltering.

"Me too." When she stares at me as if she's expecting more of an explanation, I let out a quick breath. "Way past her bedtime."

Yeo squeezes my thigh under the table. "You okay?"

Fletcher is watching me with narrowed eyes. Patty and Barclay are eerily quiet. And Dean has hardly touched his food. Gyeong and Yeo have carried the conversation the entire meal.

"I'm fine," I lie. I'm not fine. Not fine at all. I want to puke up all the delicious lasagna I managed to get down over dinner.

Barclay leans back in his chair and shoots Fletcher a look I'm not meant to interpret. But I sense the irritation and frustration and impatience rolling from him in waves. From all of them really. They want answers.

I don't have answers.

If Bones were here, he'd have answers. And insults. Hell, he'd be quite entertaining. At this, I let out a giggle. All eyes are on me—wide and confused.

"Do you remember that old camera I begged for, Dad? The one you had to have repaired for me and we spent the better part of a week listening to that old man in the shop tell us how to use the damn thing?" Yeo questions softly.

Fletcher nods, a look of understanding passing over his features, and leans forward. "It was more trouble than it was worth." His gaze is on his youngest boy—so full of pride it makes my heart hurt—and he grins at him.

Yeo chuckles. "I got better at it. Eventually. Took pictures of all of my favorite things..." he trails off and turns his gaze to me.

Everyone is quiet at the table. You could hear a pin drop. They're all letting Yeo guide the conversation. Being patient as he pulls back the layers to our love story so they can all see what hides underneath. It'll be ugly and broken to them. But to me, it's the only thing that makes sense in my world.

"I made a book," Yeo tells them, a shy smile on his lips.

Dean barks out a laugh. "Holy shit! Is this like a sex book or some crap? Are you two nymphomaniacs or something?"

Fletcher bristles at his son's outburst and shuts Dean down with a harsh glare. Then, my boyfriend's father's gaze returns to me. Encouraging. Gentle. Kind.

I stare at him blinking. The new table Yeo bought for me is unmarred. Norman's name isn't gouged out all over the surface. I was thrilled when it arrived before his family came over. I'd have been embarrassed for them to see such a terrible part of my life.

Yeo continues explaining about his camera and how he'd practice taking pictures of people and bugs but mostly me. I pick up my knife with a trembling hand. He's so animated and happy.

It should make me happy too...

But a darkness is settling over me.

A sense of foreboding.

Worry. So much worry.

What if he comes?

What if he shows up right now?

Would he storm his drunk ass around my house and

whispers and the ROARS

wreak havoc in front of Yeo's family? Worse yet, would he hurt them?

Kady. Kady. Kady.

Yeo's sweet voice parts through the cloudy haze but not quick enough. Norman's stench is here. Stale smoke and cheap liquor. My skin erupts with shivers as I feel him in the house.

Kady. Kady. Kady.

I'm torn from my present and thrust into my past.

With him.

My nightmare.

Norman.

Daddy.

"Kady," Daddy slurs as he falls face first onto my bed.

I shudder at how close he is. He stinks. Daddy always stinks. I hate how he smells. "I'm sleepy. I don't want to cuddle," I tell him bravely.

At this, he laughs darkly. Daddy's laughs are scary. I hate his laughs. His fingers tickle at my ribs. I hate his tickles. Nothing about his tickles make me laugh.

"Kady baby," he murmurs, nuzzling his nose into my hair. "You always make Daddy better, though."

I swallow and a single tear streaks down my cheek. His fingers are no longer tickling. They stroke up and down my arms in a way that used to soothe me. Now, it terrifies me. I hate his fingers.

"I don't feel good," I lie, hoping he'll leave me alone. But

143

*he never does anymore. Every night he comes into my room
so I can help him feel better.*

*"Is my nurse sick?" he slurs. "Should I be the nurse
tonight?"*

More tears roll out.

*"Let me feel your heartbeat," he murmurs, "so I can make
sure my patient is okay."*

*His fingers slip under my gown and I shudder, thankful
they bypass my panties and flutter over my chest. He grunts
behind me, pressing something hard into me. I'm afraid one
day he'll do something terrifying with that thing. Something
painful.*

*"You seem perfectly okay to me," he says. "But maybe I
should check everywhere just to be sure. Make sure you don't
have any broken bones or anything."*

I wish I could break his *bones.*

The thought, so evil and quick, has me confused.

He's my daddy. I can't hurt my daddy, can I?

But my daddy hurts me…

Please, God, help me.

"He's not my *Daddy."*

*I search my dark room for the person belonging to the
voice. Fierce but young. A boy. Brave unlike me.*

*"Who are you? Why are you in my room?" I demand,
searching the darkness. I'm embarrassed for this boy to see
the way my daddy touches me. "Please leave."*

*Daddy's fingers stop just over my belly button. "Who the
fuck are you talking to? I know you're not talking to me." His
voice is a menacing growl.*

"I'm Bones," the boy says from the shadows. "And what

your daddy is doing ain't right. Want me to stab him?"

Yes.

I want you to stab him.

"No," I lie. "Go away." *My whispered words only anger my daddy.*

"Kady..."

Kady. Kady. Kady.

I don't want to be in this room where my daddy does things that make my skin crawl. I don't want to be in this room where the boy named Bones watches what happens to me late at night when all the lights go out.

I'm sobbing with my eyes slammed shut when I hear the sounds. Slapping and hitting and grunting in anger. Bones is fighting with my daddy.

"You've lost your damn mind!" *Daddy snaps.*

I rock and murmur to myself in an attempt to fade away completely. I don't want to be here. I want to be far, far away from here.

"Go hide, Kady," *Bones tells me, his voice firm and fierce.* "I'll find you when it's over."

Minutes or hours pass, I'm not sure. But when I reopen my eyes, Daddy is gone. I flick on my lamp and am horrified to find blood on my sheets.

"I kicked him in the nose," *Bones says, his tone triumphant.*

I search for the boy, but he's hiding too well. "Where are you?"

"Always watching. Always waiting. Always wanting to help. Tonight is the first time you let me."

"I don't know you. Where are you?"

He laughs. "Right behind you, Kady. Always right behind you. I have your back."

Frightened tears roll down my cheeks. I look down at my nightgown and am thankful it's still on me. That my panties are still on my body. Bones protected me.

"Thank you."

"It was nothing," he says shyly.

I swallow and shake my head. "It was everything. You saved me from him."

The room grows quiet and I fear he left. "Bones? Please don't leave me!"

His warmth cloaks me and I can feel his smile. "I'm yours now. I'll never leave. Not ever."

chapter sixteen

Yeo

"Um, what the fuck just happened?" Barclay demands, sitting up in his seat. His face is white as a sheet.

My mother and Patty both have tears in their eyes. Dean and Dad wear matching scowls. And Barclay looks as though he may be sick.

"Norman."

My eyes flit to the table. The new table. Where he carved his name in the new wood. Everyone sat there in shock as he viciously cut into the table as he hissed out disgusting things he wanted to do to his daughter. I was too caught up in seeing his evil face to do a damn thing. Thankfully, Bones rolled in like a fucking hero, and got rid of him.

"I'm in the fucking Twilight Zone," Barclay mutters.

"Listen," I start. "Just listen."

Each pair of eyes are wide as saucers. I see the horror written all over their faces. I sense the curiosity mixed with fear radiating from them.

"Please stay. I'm going to go check on things upstairs."

Dad gives me a clipped nod that promises he'll keep them all seated and waiting. I bolt from the table and bound upstairs calling for Bones. He's not in Kady's or his room.

"Bones!" I shout as I stalk down the hallway.

A sweet voice calls out from the room at the end. "Oh, pumpkin," Agatha says when I step through the doorway. "Norman really knows how to make a mess of things."

I'm thankful to see the voice of reason in this bunch spritzing on some rose-scented perfume. She's wearing a silky floral print shirt that once belonged to Kady's grandma Ruth and a skirt. I watch as she pulls her hair into a bun and then lathers her arms up with her thick cream. Once she slides on some gaudy pearls, she then pushes her bifocals onto her face. They slide to the end of her nose where they typically sit.

"Let's go meet your family, pumpkin."

I follow behind Agatha as she shuffles down the hallway toward the stairwell. She pauses at a picture of Ruth and Kady, swipes at the dust on the top, and groans. "This house is becoming too much to keep up with in my old age. One of these days we're going to downsize."

I smile at her. "Thanks for doing this with me. You're the only one who can make them understand, I'm afraid."

She pats my arm and then loops hers around mine as we descend the stairs. Hushed whispers sound from the dining room as we round the corner. Dad's gaze flits over to Agatha. A million different expressions flit over his face: anger, sadness, confusion, and then understanding. My father understands.

"Everyone," I say, my voice husky and raw. "This is Agatha. She made the lasagna. Keeps me fed when I come to visit."

Dean nearly chokes on his water.

Barclay's eyes are as big as saucers. "What the fuck, man?"

"Language, young man," Agatha chides, pointing a long finger at him. "There are children in the house. Presley is quite the mockingbird."

Barc shoots Dad a questioning glare but Dad ignores it.

"I'm Fletcher. This is my wife and Yeo's mother, Gyeong, my boys Barclay and Dean, and my daughter-in-law, Patty. Pleasure to meet you, Agatha." He stands and strides over to her. When he takes her hand in his, Agatha blushes.

In all my years I've known her, she's never once blushed like that.

"Well, aren't you the gentleman? Yeo has told me nothing but lovely things about you, Fletcher. About you all in fact," Agatha says with a broad smile. "I see the lasagna was to your satisfaction?"

Barc groans and pats his belly as if just now remembering how he ate three helpings.

"Please, have a seat." I motion to Kady's place. Agatha walks over and sits. Her eyes flit down to the new kitchen table that's been scarred with Norman's name and she frowns.

"That rat bastard," she hisses.

I've never heard the woman swear. She's pissed.

"He made an appearance. Bones ran him off."

Her eyes scan the group. Everyone is fascinated by Agatha. "I do apologize. Kady was worried he'd show up. The girl is already so terrible at social gatherings. I know she was terrified something bad would happen and you all would hate her. Please don't hate what isn't her fault. Kady is a good girl." Agatha's eyes, which look huge behind her bifocals, drop to her lap. "Once you all understand her, I pray to our Lord, you all will grow to love her. Kady has had a rough life. She deserves a happy one. This boy here is the only person I know who makes her smile and forget her past."

Dad clenches his jaw. My mother and Patty are speechless.

"Why don't you show them the book while I dish up the pie, pumpkin," Agatha urges as she stands back up. "Anyone want coffee while I'm up?"

Dean mutters something about needing a stiff drink but is silenced when Dad waves his snide comment off. "I'd love a cup. Gyeong will have some tea if you have it, Agatha."

Agatha blushes again and nods. "Certainly."

When she's out of earshot, Dad snaps his head over to my brothers. "Enough." Then, his eyes find mine. "Let's see the book."

Swallowing, I walk over to the hutch where the book sits. It took a long time to create the book. Many pictures. Many years. Many confusing moments that still don't make a whole lot of sense.

I pick it up. It's a scrapbook of sorts. Not terribly thick but it explains so much. I set it down in front of my dad.

Everyone cranes their necks to see what I have to share. Opening it, I turn to the first page.

"You are terrifying and strange and beautiful, something not everyone knows how to love."

Warsan Shires's words in my messy teenage writing says everything. That quote *is* my Kady.

"This is officially getting creepy," Barc groans. Patty swats at him and he quiets down.

I flip open to the first page.

Kady.

Messy brown hair. Bright blue eyes. A secretive smile on her face. At sixteen, she was every bit as beautiful as she is now. The girl in the picture is my Kady. The girl I've chased and loved since I was ten years old. *I love her.*

"What I'm about to show you is going to hurt or be confusing but I need you to stay with me. Please," I urge.

Flipping the page, I hold my breath.

Bones.

Messy brown hair. Bright blue eyes. A wicked smile on his face. At sixteen, he was every bit as naughty as he is now. The boy in the picture is my Bones. The boy who's been there with her through it all. *I love him.*

"What the fuck? Why are you showing us this?" Dean demands. His eyes linger on Bones's bare chest in the picture and it's far from sexual. It's confusion. Bones has a joint between his lips in the picture and a package of Cheetos on his belly.

"That's Bones," I murmur. "Bones is my best friend—Kady's best friend. And he's…"

All eyes meet mine in question.

"He's an avenger alter."

Agatha clangs around in the kitchen and I swallow.

Flipping to the next page, I smile.

Agatha.

Neat brown hair pulled into a bun. Bright blue eyes hidden behind bifocals. A kind, gentle smile on her face. The woman in the picture is my Agatha. *I love her.*

"This is fucked up," Barc murmurs.

Dad speaks, his voice a hushed whisper. "Go on."

I turn the page and chuckle.

Presley.

Cute brown pigtails. Wide blue eyes. A crooked, sticky grin on her face. The girl in the picture is my Presley. *I love her.*

"Presley," Dad murmurs. "From the ice cream shop."

Mom's face is sad and tears well in her eyes. She pats my Dad's shoulder.

"Agatha is a protective alter. Presley is a child alter," I explain.

"Dude," Barclay says softly, "what this hell is this?"

"Is she a schizo or some shit?" Dean questions.

Swallowing down my anger at his rude generalization, I shake my head. "Schizophrenia is a disease more complicated than my Kady's. She doesn't hallucinate or have delusions. Kady has Dissociative Identity Disorder. You may know it as Multiple Personality Disorder."

Everyone, including myself, lets out a collective breath of air.

I continue. "This disorder, although extremely rare, is brought on by severe traumatic events to help the person cope with whatever heinous thing they've been forced to endure. Kady was sexually and physically abused as a child by her father. Norman. Eventually, she witnessed her own father brutally murder her mother." Glancing over at his newly carved name, I shudder with rage. Patty starts to cry as realization sinks in. "Bones was her first alter. Her mind created him to help her escape and cope with what Norman did to her. Bones has been protecting her ever since."

When I flip the page, I laugh. Whiskers is sitting on the countertop in the picture lapping at warm milk. The only cat I'm not allergic to. Lazy blue eyes and one of those arrogant kitty smirks on his face. He's my cat. *I love him.*

"Sometimes these alters aren't the host's same sex or even species. They're called non-human alters. Whiskers is a black and orange tabby cat. He's old and spoiled. Loves when you scratch behind his ears," I explain.

"How many of these alters does she have?" Dad asks. His eyebrows are drawn together as he attempts to understand.

"Nine."

The room is silent as I flip the page.

"Aunt Suzy. She's like an aunt. Suzy is an extreme coupon cutter. It is my understanding that Suzy is the mother Kady never really had. Her own mother was a shell and under her father's thumb until he squashed her once and for all. Suzy is the one who shops for the family and runs errands."

"Family," Dean murmurs. "But it's just the one. The one person living here. Kady."

Gritting my teeth, I nod. "They all work like a family.

Each one knows about the other. They don't actively talk to each other in her head or anything from what I've gathered—although I'm not exactly sure about that. Agatha developed a note system for them. Notepads can be found all over the house. It's how they communicate effectively. One of the alters I know for sure can directly communicate with her, though."

"Bones." Dad is paying attention I can see.

"Yes," I tell him. "They still leave each other notes but they can speak to one another from time to time."

I'm about to flip the page when Agatha comes shuffling in passing out plates of pie. This time, they all regard her with new eyes. Eyes of understanding although they're more curious now.

"This is delicious, Agatha," Mom says, complimenting the old woman.

Agatha smiles at her. "Thank you, sweetheart. Would you like some cream and sugar for your tea?"

I remain still beside my father as Agatha flits about the dining room making sure everyone is cared for. Once she settles in Kady's chair, I flit my gaze her way. She nods and gives me an encouraging smile.

"Go on, pumpkin. Tell them about our girl."

"This is Officer Joe," I tell them, pointing at the figure staring back, dark aviator shades over his eyes. He's serious and stern but protective as can be. "He's also a protective alter. After Norman killed her mother, Officer Joe was at her side promising to keep her safe. He comes around to check on her. And he also helps keep *them* away so they won't hurt her."

Dad's gaze snaps to mine, anger working his jaw muscles. "Who's them?"

"Kenneth," I say with a hiss as I flip the page, "is what they call a self-destroyer alter. He's depressed and self harms." I can't even look at his face. In the picture, he's staring at the knife in his hand as he runs it across his thigh. Once I left for college, his preference of self-harm was cigarette burns on the inside of his thighs.

The scars on Kady's legs—scars he put there—make me quake with rage.

"Fuck." Barclay's one word just voices everyone else's thoughts.

Turning another page, I groan. "Pascale. He's a drug addicted loser. A fucking thug."

"Language, Yeo," Agatha chides. She's not too angry, though. She hates Pascale too.

With a sigh, I turn to Dean. "Pascale hangs out with the wrong crowd. He carries a gun and deals drugs. He's dangerous to Kady. I don't like how he drags her to God knows where to do God knows what. He's a persecutor alter."

"You learned all of this in med school?" Dad questions, awe in his voice.

"The technical stuff, yes. But I didn't need a textbook to explain that Kady was all of these different people in one body. When I was introduced to Bones by her grandma, I knew. I'd somehow wiggled my way into her world and there was no getting out. I didn't want to get out. I needed to know them all because..."

"They're all her," Dad says softly.

Nodding, I turn the page. As soon as I see his face, I

seethe with rage. "You met this asshole tonight," I growl. "Norman. Her fucking father."

Dean lets out a huff. "You mean to tell me one of her alters is her dad? How in the hell does that shit happen?"

Running my fingers through my hair, I shrug. "I don't know. Norman came onto the scene after Louise died. The real Norman is in prison for life. But he'd become such an evil in her life. She's mentally worked so hard to protect herself from him through the years, creating alter after alter, that when he was finally gone from her life, Norman came back. This time, as a persecuting alter. One she'll never get away from." I sigh in frustration. Mom squeezes my hand to comfort me.

"She needs help," Patty murmurs.

I snap my gaze to her and glare. "She has help. She has me. I've always been there to help exorcise the bad ones from her. But she loves the good ones. The good ones protect her and shield her from all that hurts her. At dinner last week, you all were the ones hurting her. It was Bones who came to her rescue and saved her. Kady doesn't need help—not from some institution. They'll only dope her up with meds that aren't going to work. Kady just needs love. She needs me and Bones and Agatha. She needs her alters she's befriended. Together, we drive away the darkness in her mind. Together, we are her light."

Agatha shifts uncomfortably in her seat. "Who wants seconds?" she sings but I sense her unease despite the sing-song voice.

Everyone turns to look at her, their gazes assessing the old woman. To me, I see Agatha. They're all so different from one another. Each alter. But it's the world who doesn't know Kady that seems to have trouble adjusting.

Kady is still beautiful hiding beneath the old lady glasses. Her perfect breasts can be seen through the floral blouse. Those plump lips now caked with an orangey colored lipstick were all over my cock just hours ago.

But despite her looking like Kady in an old woman's disguise, it's not her. The beautiful woman before me is Agatha. Agatha is her own person.

"How do you keep the bad ones away?" Dad asks, his eyes darting over to Agatha as he pushes his empty pie plate toward her.

She beams at him and collects it to fetch him more pie.

"Bones and I do it. He works from the inside and I work on the outside. I don't exactly know what he does inside her head but he scares them. Bones can be..." I smile. "Unconventional."

"You love him," Patty whispers, her voice dumfounded.

I think of Bones. My best friend stuck inside my girlfriend's body. Fucked up. When he tatted his nipple with my name, he tatted hers. He tatted Agatha and Presley and the fucking cat.

"I do. I love most of her alters in some way."

"What do you do?" Dad asks. "On the 'outside.'"

I sigh and pace beside the table. "I try not to physically hurt them. Only intimidate them. Sometimes things do get physical." Regret shreds my voice. My eyes flicker to Agatha's neck as she reenters the room with Dad's pie. A yellowish fading bruise colors the side of her neck. A bruise I'd given to Pascale when I put him in a choke hold so he wouldn't shoot my ass.

"But you do hurt them sometimes?" Dad questions with a growl as he takes it from her.

"Bones and I do what we can to stop them from ulti-mately hurting Kady. If that means physically restraining them or on occasion having to knock them out, it's what I do. I'm not proud, Dad, of having to do that shit but I have to. Because if I don't keep them from hurting her, one of them will kill her. Kenneth scares the hell out of me be-cause one day I'm afraid he's going to cut open her wrists and I won't be there to keep it from happening."

Agatha senses my upset and rushes over to me. She hugs my middle. "You're doing great, pumpkin. The book you made helps them see. It's hard to see but they're getting it. They truly are."

"How old are you?" Mom asks Agatha.

"Sixty-eight," Agatha says. "Kady and Bones and Yeo are like grandchildren to me. I'd be lost without them."

Mom smiles and reaches her hand for Agatha who takes it without hesitation. "Thank you for looking out for my boy." Agatha nods and then excuses herself from the room.

Dad polishes off another piece of pie and then leans back in his seat. His brows are furrowed together in a scowl. "So who takes care of her?"

I bristle at his question. "I do."

"For twelve years you didn't. You were in school. Who looks after her and makes sure she doesn't hurt herself or that one of her alters don't hurt her?" I know he's not at-tacking me but I can't help but grow defensive. "Yeo, I know you don't want to hear this but she needs round the clock care."

Gritting my teeth, I snarl at him. "I'm here now. I'm not going anywhere ever again. She ran me off hoping I'd find someone better. I didn't want anyone better. I wanted her. So I went to school so I could help her. I studied every mental illness known to man but I especially studied hers. We're together now. Everything is going to be okay."

"But what about when you have to work or leave town for business? What about when you sleep or run errands? Who takes care of her then? You can't drag her around town with you wherever you go. This is too large of a burden for you to bear alone, son." His eyes are pained. Pained for both Kady and I. My heart sinks in my chest.

"I don't bear it alone. They help me."

Dean shoots Barclay an exasperated look. "Her other personalities help you."

"Yes," I growl. "While I was in college, I talked to them on the phone and kept track. They love her and don't want anything to happen to her."

Dad speaks, his voice resigned. "You, of all people since you studied medicine, should realize she needs help outside of your abilities."

Fisting my hands at my sides, I growl at him. "I'm able to help her better than anyone because I love her, Dad. I brought you all here so you could understand her, not give you more ammunition to try and drag me away from her."

"Whoa, Kitty Muncher," Bones says with a laugh from behind me. "What's got your panties in a wad?"

As much as I love Bones, now's not the time.

Turning to regard him, I cringe. He's typical Bones wearing nothing but a pair of low slung jeans that hang from his hips and no shirt. To me, he's just my friend. To them, he's a half-naked Kady acting strangely.

"Dear God," Dad murmurs.

Ignoring them, Bones saunters into the dining room and plops down in Kady's chair. His fingertip runs along Norman's name carved into the wood. With a grumble, he looks up at me. "That fucker is in hiding. Punk ass child molester."

Dean is gawking at Bones's chest. Both of my parents and Patty have chosen to look elsewhere.

"Where's Agatha?" Dad questions, his discomfort evident.

Bones smirks. "She sent me in here to deal with you fuckers. Said shit was gettin' intense in here. Said you all were about to drag Kitty Muncher out of here if I didn't come down here and intervene. Well here I am," he says and winks at Dean, grabbing his crotch salaciously. "Motherfucking intervening. I'm fucking hungry. What are we eating?"

When Barclay starts laughing, clearly amused at Bones's behavior, I tense. "You've got to be kidding me right now. What is even happening around here? It's a mad house here. Yeo, bro, I'm fucking exhausted and I've only been here an hour. How do you keep your own head sane after all these years?"

I'm about to speak up when Bones rises from his chair. "Shut your fucking mouth, dog." His entire body quakes with protective rage. Protective over me. It warms me that he's standing up for me.

"Dog?" Barclay hisses and stands.

"Woof," Bones taunts.

Barclay's face burns bright red as he glares at him.

"Dude, calm the hell down," Dean gripes and jerks our brother back into his seat. "You're picking a fight with a girl."

Wrong words.

Fuck.

"What did you call me?" Bones seethes.

Dean's gaze drops to Bones tattooed chest and he laughs. "I called you a girl because you are. If you'd drop your pants right now, we'd all have our proof and—"

Dean doesn't get another word in before Bones scrambles up on the table and attacks my brother. My brother doesn't have a chance against my best friend because one is crazy while the other is not. One has no boundaries. One will claw his heart out and feed it to him for dinner. Bones's fist makes contact three quick, furious times before I jolt out of my frozen stance. Sliding my arm around him, I drag him away from my brother and out of the dining room. I can hear Dad bitching my brothers out as I haul Bones up the stairs to his room. He fights and squirms, ready for a fight but I'm stronger and don't let go.

Not until I've slammed the door behind us and pushed him against it.

"Calm the fuck down, Bones," I order, my breaths coming out in quick succession.

His eyes are dilated with rage. He'd wanted to hurt my brother. For me. Bones always looks after Kady because she needs it. It makes me realize just how much he looks after me too.

"Look at me," I demand.

He meets my gaze and it softens slightly. "Fucking assholes, those two."

"You're just mad because Kady's upset. Because Norman made an appearance. Chill out, man."

"You tried and fucking failed," he seethes. "They just don't get her. They don't get us."

Leaning forward, I rest my forehead against his. "They don't matter. I get her and you and Agatha and all the rest. That's all that matters."

He pulls his hand from my grip and slides it down my chest to my slacks. When he grips me, my cock jolts to life at his touch. "That night," he murmurs and squeezes my dick, "we both know it wasn't the last time. There will never be a last anything between us."

I groan and let my lips crush his. He kisses me like Kady kisses me. With love. "Fuck, Bones. You're so damn difficult."

He laughs as he slides to the floor on his knees. The moment he frees my cock and slips his hot mouth over it, I'm a goner. So much for last times. So much for closure. I'll never rid my heart of this man. He filled a void when Kady hid from me, and now, I'll be fucking empty if he ever leaves that hole in my heart.

"Bones," I mutter as I fist his hair. "I love you."

And not because he's practically swallowing my dick. I love him because he's been there for us both since the beginning. I love him because he's crazy and fucked up and my best friend.

His teeth scrape against my shaft in such an exhilarating way, I find myself tilting my head back and groaning in pleasure. The desire to come is overwhelming. When his mouth hums a bit with a small moan, I lose control.

The heat from my orgasm explodes from me and drains deep into his throat. He swallows every drop. As soon as my dick stops twitching, he pops off of it, making an obscene sound loud enough I fear my family may have heard. When he rises, he wipes his chin off with the back of his hand and flashes me a salacious grin that barely hides his true feelings for me.

"Back at ya, Kitty Muncher."

In Bones's words...*I love you too.*

chapter seventeen

Kady

"Wake up."

A deep voice rumbles me awake and I sit up, rubbing sleep out of my eyes. As soon as my eyes focus, I realize we're in a dark room that smells of weed. "Why are we in Bones's bed?"

Yeo grins at me and runs his fingertip down along my ribs toward my hipbone. "This is where the night took us."

Rolling my eyes at his answer, I flicker my gaze over to the nightstand. A bottle of lube sits on top beside a condom wrapper. My eyes find Yeo's and I know. They had sex.

"Is he happy?" I wonder aloud. Bones is never truly happy. The closest he's ever become is when he's been with Yeo.

"I think so." Yeo's black eyebrows furrow together. His handsome face is twisted up as if he's in pain. "Are you mad?"

Blinking at him several times, I try to harness the

feeling in my heart. Is it anger or jealousy? No. I feel...*glad*.

Bones deserves to be happy.

Bones deserves so much more than I could ever give him.

"Do you love him?"

"Like I love you," he admits. His fingers rake through the hair at my temple and his thumb slides over my cheekbone. "I seem to always hurt him. I'm tired of hurting him."

My heart aches at the way Bones has felt lately. Ever since Yeo came back. The longing in his heart hurts—physically hurts—me. But when Yeo gives in to him and gives Bones what he desperately craves—physical connection and affection and sex—he's content and satisfied. His heart is filled with love. A love I both recognize and share.

"I don't want Bones to hurt either."

He leans forward and presses a soft kiss to my nose. "We've never really made sense to anyone, you and I, but to me we make perfect sense. And somehow, Bones fits into our mess. It's always been the three of us in some way, shape, or form."

"So what's going to happen now?"

When he doesn't answer, I lean forward and kiss him softly to urge him on.

"I don't know. I suppose we'll just make it work," he says with a sigh.

His words fill me with hope. If Bones could be happy right along with us, then that would make me happy too.

"You're my girl," he whispers. I like it when he whispers. "And he's my best friend."

I smile. "The Terrible Three."

He chuckles at the nickname Grandma gave us. "I don't suppose it will ever be any other way."

This morning felt…normal.

Such an odd word.

Not at all something I'm familiar with.

Now that Yeo's back, my cloudy world seems more clear. I find that I'm myself more lately than not. For once in a really long time, I'm not so tired. Hiding from what scares me is a full-time job. A job I can never take a break from. But with Yeo? I can at least take a moment to breathe and just be Kady.

A smile tugs at my lips as I gather Bones's dirty clothes, which are scattered about his bedroom. Normally Agatha does the washing, but I want to do something nice for her today. She stayed with Yeo as he explained my afflictions to his family. I can't thank her enough. Laundry is the least I can do.

When Yeo left this morning, my heart ached a bit, but I knew he wouldn't be gone long. And now that Bones senses Yeo isn't leaving him, his satisfaction hangs thick in the air. Things are beginning to look up. I wish I would have never asked Yeo to leave me in the first place. I missed out on him for twelve long years.

I scoop up the half-full laundry basket and head down the hallway. I'm always careful to avoid *her* room. The room where nightmares are born. The room where Norman now resides. Normally, we all manage to keep that room locked up. It's a place none of us like to go. We all hate my mother's old room. A shiver quivers through me when I see the door is cracked open. Sometimes Whiskers goes in there to lie in front of the big window where the sun pours in. I'm about to scold the old cat when memories begin latching their thick tendrils around the sane part of my mind. Those wicked memories drag me into the darkness and I immediately begin to drown in them.

Voices.

Whispered hisses that slowly become roars.

They're not in my head this time. This time they're real. The voices don't come from Grandma or Yeo. They don't come from Bones or Presley. They come from Mommy. And him.

When something crashes, fear laces around my heart and squeezes painfully. I slip out of bed and tiptoe toward my bedroom door. After I tug it open, I hear the voices more clearly.

"You're not supposed to be here, Norman." Mommy's voice is wobbly.

"She's my daughter. I miss her," he seethes. He hisses something I can't hear, which makes her cry harder.

Scrambling down the hallway, I make my way to Mommy's bedroom. The door is ajar and I can see shadows moving around in the darkened room.

"You hurt her," Mommy says in a fierce tone. "I can't let you hurt her anymore. Leave before I call the cops. I'm

not yours to destroy anymore." I've never heard her sound so brave before. I'm aching to run and hug her. To tell her how proud I am of her.

But I'm scared.

What if he gets me?

"Kady, go back to bed," Bones says with a grumble from behind me. "If he sees you…"

I turn to look for my friend. I don't see him. I never see him. But I always hear him.

"What if he hurts Mommy again?" I ask tearfully.

Bones's warmth cloaks me from behind. I feel comforted and safe with him behind me. "What if he hurts you again?"

A cold, sick feeling pours over me. It reminds me of how we watched that science video in class. The seagulls that had become covered in oil from a spill in the ocean. How the slippery black substance was glued to their tiny bodies. No way to get it off except to scrub and scrub and scrub.

I wish someone would scrub the feeling off of me.

Daddy is dirty and scary.

He poisons me from the outside.

One day I want to be completely clean again. Just like the gulls after the volunteers wash away the grime. But who will help me wash it all away?

Big brown eyes.

Black, straight hair.

Crooked grin.

Yeo.

Yeo will wash it all away. I'm his Kadydid. He's my friend. A real friend.

"I'm real too," Bones grunts, *offended by my thoughts.*

I smile. "I know, silly."

Something crashes in Mommy's room making both Bones and I jump.

"Go back to bed, Kady," he urges, a slight panicked tone in his voice. Bones is never scared. If Bones is frightened, I should be terrified.

"But Mommy..."

"Go!"

Bones roars sometimes.

His roars make me run.

Bones

As soon as Kady scampers off into the shadows, I fist my hands and charge into her momma's bedroom. Fear threatens to tear my chest in half but it's my duty to protect Kady. She's so small and so innocent. Her stupid daddy tries to hurt her. I hate him.

"Well, well, well," Norman's deep voice growls. "And who do we have here?" A lamp turns on and I see his giant form looming beside the bed. Kady's daddy looks bigger than he did the last time we saw him. His eyes are darker and wild. By the way he sways, I know he's drunk.

"Please leave," Louise begs through her tears. "Momma will wake up and she'll call the police. They'll haul you away."

Norman laughs, the sound evil and sinister. If I didn't have Kady to protect, I'd run and hide from it.

"You better go before you get hurt," I threaten, squaring

my shoulders. "I will fucking gut you." Kady's grandma would make me bite on the soap bar if she'd heard that f-bomb.

Tears stream down Louise's bright red cheeks. Understanding flickers in her eyes. "Bones, go. Please, just go to Kady's room and lock the door."

"Bones?" Norman jerks his gaze to her. "So she is a schitzo just like I fucking knew. Is she channeling our dead son?" he hisses when he meets my furious gaze. "Huh? You pretending to be our Kenneth. Newsflash, ya dumb shit, you don't have a dick. You'll never be the son we lost."

Louise charges at him and attempts to shove him. He's too large for her tiny frame. Easily, he slings his arm back and elbows her right in the face. Her nose makes a popping sound and she crumples to the ground letting out a pained moan. With a rage filled roar, I charge for him, my fists tight and ready to pummel. I manage to get one punch to his solid stomach before he grabs my throat.

"So you're a boy? Is that right?" he snarls, lifting me up to where my toes barely touch the wood floors. I gasp for air and claw at his thick wrist.

He squeezes and sneers at me. My vision goes black for a moment. "Boys don't wear pink nightgowns. Unless they're gay. Are you gay, Bones?" His tone is mocking.

My fight has left me as I focus slowly on gasping for air that seems to be locked right above his grip in my throat.

"Bones!" Kady is crying for me somewhere.

Go away, Kady.

Hide, Kady.

Don't watch this, Kady.

I may not be able to talk but she hears. Kady always

hears.

"You know what happens to gay boys?" Norman demands, spittle showering my face. He tosses me onto the bed and I gasp for air like a fish out of water, clutching at my sore neck. "They take it up the ass!"

"Bones!" Kady's sobs are my only focus.

"Run, Kady!" I hiss out, my voice a hoarse whisper. "He can't hurt you anymore!"

Norman's murderous gaze meets mine and he pounces before I can move. He manhandles me onto my stomach and presses his disgusting erection against my butt through the fabric of the stupid nightgown I'm wearing. I wish I had jeans on.

"You're Kady," he says with a cruel laugh. "My little princess."

I squirm and desperately attempt to get out of his hold. "She's gone. Do your worst, asshole, but she won't know what you've done. I'll protect her."

He growls as he yanks my underwear down. I close my eyes and focus on Yeo—my and Kady's best friend. I think about how his cheeks turn bright red when I cuss in front of Kady's grandma Ruth. I think about how he's always got a package of Cheetos for me whenever he comes to visit. I think about how badly he sucks at Monopoly. I think about the time he hugged me when I fell off Kady's bike and skinned both knees. I'd been embarrassed and told him to leave me alone, but he didn't. Yeo stuck by my side. Yeo is always by our side.

Like now.

Norman can do terrible things to me, but I have the

ability to block it out. To replace the terror and physical pain with something perfect. Something beautiful. Yeo.

"Such a good boy, Bones," Norman taunts, *dragging me away from a smiling Yeo in my mind.* "Just like our Kenneth would have been if he'd ever been born."

Pain rips through me, but I quickly drag my awareness away from the present and back into the memories. Memories from this morning when Yeo and I ate popsicles on the front porch.

Norman is weak.

He can't hurt Kady anymore.

And he certainly can't hurt me.

I'm Bones.

Strong. Resilient. Unbreakable.

Kady

I'm dragged back to the present when I hear his voice.

"Don't go in there," Bones says, his voice a firm command.

A shudder ripples through me. "Why is the door open? Was Norman here?"

Inhaling a lingering scent of beer, I know that he must have been. The urge to call Yeo is strong. To beg him to hurry home and keep the monsters away.

"I'll keep the monsters away too, you know," Bones murmurs, a slight bit of sadness in his tone.

Swallowing, I nod as I reach for the door handle to

close it. I can't help but peek into my mother's old bedroom with one hand on the knob. The bloodstain never came out of the wood floors no matter how many times Grandma attempted to clean them. She'd even tried to refinish the wood to no avail. Closing the door to those memories is how she and I'd handled the terror of losing my mother.

"I wish I would have killed him that night," Bones hisses. I can feel his warmth on the back of my neck as he also peers into the bedroom. "If only I'd gone in there prepared. I could have stabbed him. Jesus, Kady, I should have gut that fucker right then and there. Then, he'd have never come back the next weekend."

I smile at his ferocity but it quickly falls away. "He hurt you. Grandma had to take you to the emergency room. Daddy was stronger than you." A tear streaks down my cheek and I almost drop the laundry basket I'm barely gripping under one arm. The damage to Bones's anus had mostly been superficial and only required a couple of stitches. He was so tough about it. Never let me in on the details of the pain he endured that week while he healed. I'd once again hidden and let Bones deal with the horrible stuff alone. "I'm sorry, Bones. I'm sorry I brought you into this unfair world. I'm sorry you had to help me fight my battles." I begin to sob. Closing my eyes, I relish in the way Bones's love for me seems to envelop me in a warm hug. "I wish I were stronger."

"I *chose* to fight those battles for you, babe. I'll be here until you don't need me anymore," he murmurs. I hate how sad he sounds. How it seems to bleed from him. How it fills the room and threatens to drown me in his sorrow.

"I'll always need you," I tell him firmly. "Always."

Bones whispers against my ear. I love his whispers. "Not always."

chapter eighteen

Yeo

"Tell me your plan, son." Dad's fingers are steepled together, a greying eyebrow arched in question.

I run my fingers through my hair, messing up the gel, and shrug. "The plan is...there is no plan."

He sighs in frustration.

"You can't plan when it comes to Kady," I quickly rush out. "You saw how she truly is at dinner. You all did."

Mom gives me a reassuring smile. After I left Kady this morning, I came over to my parents' house for breakfast and to discuss what happened last night.

"She's sick." My dad's jaw is set tight and he scowls. But despite his words, I see behind his gruff exterior. He understands her now. And he wants to help her.

"I know. But listen," I say, meeting his hard gaze. "I've gone to med school. I've done rotations in the psych ward. I've interviewed countless doctors and professors. Dad, I've spent every waking hour that I wasn't studying or interning researching Kady's mental illness. There aren't medicines to magically make all the voices go away. She can't simply go to an institution where they'll fix her with extreme therapies. The only thing we can do is accept her the way she is. These alters she's created are a part of her. They've been a part of her for some time. It isn't something that will just go away. Kady isn't someone to be cured. This is her."

My father, ever the problem solver, frowns. He flits his gaze over to my mother's briefly before coming back to mine. "Agatha and Presley. They seem sweet. Bones is protective. That much I can tell. But..." he trails off. His face darkens to crimson as rage sets in. "Norman. He isn't good. We all watched as he cut his name into her brand new table. We all had to listen as he hissed out those terrible things he wanted to do to her."

"Bless her," Mom mutters over her tea and sniffles.

I swallow and nod. "Norman can be driven away. I just need to make that happen. It will happen," I assure him.

His lips press into a thin line. "Yeo..."

I straighten my back. I can tell by the look on his face I'm not going to like what he has to say.

"You know you'll never be able to have a normal marriage or children. You do understand this, right? There's no way you could bring a child into that environment," he says sadly.

Inhaling a deep breath, I meet his gaze. "I know. In fact, she and I both know. It's not something we want. I don't need children with Kady to be happy. I just need Kady."

Mom reaches over and pats my arm. "She needs you too."

My heart aches in my chest and I give her a thankful smile before turning back to Dad. "All I'm asking is for your support. Not financial or anything like that. I need your love and guidance. I need to know that when things get hard, I have you two and the rest of my family to fall back on. To assist when I can't be everywhere at once."

Dad sighs and takes a long sip of his coffee. "How will you be able to manage a practice and care for Kady full time?"

"I called Kush on the way over here. He's made the decision, despite his father's wishes, to move to Morgantown. I've been friends with him since my early days at Yale. Kush is hardworking and trustworthy. If I have a partner, he can see patients when I can't. We'll make it work," I assure him.

His eyes narrow at me and I see the businessman, not my dad, considering my words. After a long moment, he gives me a small smile. "You've thought a lot about this."

Nodding, I make sure to meet his stare with a firm one of my own. "It's all I've thought about since I graduated high school. For twelve years, I've planned this life for Kady and I. It's been a long road. We've come this far and it will only get better. You'll see. When I'm with Kady, she's mostly Kady. Her alters tend to fade into the background. Some hardly show up at all. Especially the bad ones. I can help her have the best life she'll ever hope to have. I'll do anything for her, Dad. I've done everything for her."

He pulls his phone from his breast pocket and dials someone. When they answer, he launches into what he has to say. So Dad. No time for pleasantries. "Rita, tell Rick we want to purchase the building on Second street downtown."

His eyes meet mine for a moment and I see resignation in them. He knows this is the only way. I need my family on my side, not against me. "Yes, cash. Like he and I had talked about. Mmmhhm," he says and I can hear her chattering on the other end. "Yes. Soon as possible. I'd like to take ownership over the property by the end of the month. Thank you."

"Thanks, Dad," I tell him, my voice full of relief.

"Of course," he grunts as if it's no big deal. But it is a huge deal. "Now what will she do while you work? You can't keep up with her all the time, son."

"She'll come with me. Between Kush and I, we'll make sure she has things to do that she's capable of. Things that won't interfere with our patients. We'll think of something. Not to mention"—I scrub my face and let out a breath—"she can get some much-needed therapy. When Kush gets here, I'll have her meet with him. I'm hoping she'll like him enough to sit with him."

Dad's eyebrows are raised in surprise. "You really have thought of everything. Do you think Kady will participate in the therapies? What if one of the alters decides they don't want to go along with it?"

Several of her alters are difficult and dangerous. I'm hoping Bones and I can get rid of them. The rest love Kady. The other alters will participate because they love me too.

"Bones and I will make sure of it."

My phone buzzes in my pocket. As soon as I read the text from Kady's number, the blood in my veins grows cold.

Kady: Kitty Muncher, it's me. Bones. She's upset about Louise's door having been left open. She only acts

this way when Kenneth is coming. I need your help.

I'm out the door without so much as a goodbye to my parents.

"KADY!" I bellow from the bottom of her stairwell before charging two at a time up the steps. "BONES!"

The house is eerily silent and I panic. That fucker better not be here. Goddammit!

I'm headed down the hallway toward Kady's room when I see Louise's door ajar. When I push through, I almost lose my fucking mind.

Kenneth.

I know this because his weapon of choice is gripped firmly in his hand.

Naked and sitting cross legged on the bed.

Kenneth loves his weapons.

I'd recognize his destructive self from a mile away.

"Bones!" I yell at Kenneth, hoping to reach him.

Kenneth lazily raises his impassive gaze to mine. Blood runs down the inside of his thighs. He's been slicing what seems to be words amongst the already cigarette burn scarred flesh.

"What have you done?" I seethe, my body tense and poised to pounce. I'm afraid to move though in case he digs the razorblade in too deep. "That's not your body to destroy."

He lifts his droopy gaze to mine and frowns. Kenneth is always in another world. Every time he sees me it's as if

I'm a figment of his imagination. Confusion sets in and his hand holding the razorblade begins to tremble. "Get out of my head! All of you!"

"It's you who needs to go," I growl as I take a slow step toward him. "Give me the razorblade."

His dark brown brows furrow together and he begins murmuring to himself as if to drive away my words. The moment he brings the blade back down toward his thigh, I launch at him. Grabbing his wrist, I tackle him onto the bed and pin the offending arm down. He grunts and wriggles beneath me, but I'm stronger.

I'm stronger than all of them.

"Bones…" I hiss into face.

I manage to peel the blade from Kenneth's grip and toss it to the floor. Then, I wrangle him onto his belly. With my heavier body, I keep him pinned to the bed until one of the others takes over.

"Agatha? Kady? Aunt Suzy?"

Kenneth continues to fight me but he'll never get loose.

"We can do this all day, Kenneth. Give up."

When he grows quiet and quits moving, I let out a sigh of relief. I hate that he smells like her. That his body is hers. That he hurts her.

"Kady," I murmur against Kenneth's bare shoulder. "Come back to me, Kadydid."

I press a kiss to his flesh hoping to draw her back to me. And then another kiss. And another.

Please come back to me.

While I wait, I drift to happier times.

I like to kiss the smooth skin between her ample breasts. Always warm and so sweet. It's my favorite part of her. Like it was made just for me.

"How much will it cost me to rent this pretty little piece of real estate?" I question before tonguing a trail between her tits toward her belly button.

She giggles—oh-so-sweet—and I grin. "It's free."

I nip at her belly button. "Free? What did I do to get such a good deal, beautiful?"

"Everything," she murmurs, her fingers threading into my hair.

My mouth presses hot kisses down toward her perfect pussy. Her grandma is away at the grocery store so we have a good hour before she comes back. The things I can do in an hour…

"I want to give you more than everything," I tell her, my mouth hovering over her sex. When I look up, she's watching me with hooded eyes. Her perfect tits heave with every breath she takes.

"You're all I need."

I drop a kiss onto her lips—the ones situated on either side of her clit—and revel in the kitten-like mewl she lets out. When my tongue flicks out and I run it along her slit, she grips my hair like she's contemplating yanking it all out.

"Yeo!"

Our eyes meet again. Fire blazes in her gorgeous gaze. I love when I get one-hundred percent Kady. The more time we spend together, the more I see just her. Sure, the others come to visit from time to time, but not like they do when we're forced apart. Last year, Dad took Mom and I to visit South Korea. When I returned three weeks later, Kady was overrun by her alters.

Alters.

That's what I learned they are called.

I've googled what I can about her and one day I hope to learn more.

"Oh God!" she cries out, dragging me from my thoughts. "Don't stop!"

Like I could stop even if I wanted to.

When it comes to Kady, all I do is go, go, go.

Kenneth grunts in my grip, dragging me back to the present, and I hold him tighter. I know I need to tend to the wounds he's inflicted on Kady's thighs but first Bones and I have to take care of him. Whatever Bones does from the inside works. He's done it before and I have no doubts he'll do it again.

Come on, Bones.

Run this twisted prick out of our girl's head once and for all.

chapter nineteen

Bones

I t's motherfuckin' show time.

Operation: Get Those Fuckers Outta Her Head—
Starting with Kenneth.

Kitty Muncher is doing his part. Doing what he does best. Drawing Kady out and forcing Kenneth back in. Shoving that piece of shit back into the darkness with the rest of us hood rats.

"I'm not a hood rat, pumpkin," Agatha kindly reminds me. "I'm not even sure I know what one is."

Yeah, yeah…

"Presley, glasses," I order as I tug my black Nirvana shirt off my ripped-as-fuck body. Bones my ass. Only when I get to drive around in Kady's world. When I'm in here, *in my world*, I'm the motherfuckin' king. Biggest badass around.

"Pink or black?" she questions, her cute nose scrunched up. Whiskers, that fat cat, squirms in her arms but she has a death grip on the poor fuck.

I pretend to think for a moment before settling on the black pair. Smirking at her, I slip the sunglasses on and run my fingers through my crazy dark hair.

"Agatha, Cheetos."

She snorts in response but I hear the familiar crackling before she holds up a cheesy treat in my view. I pop one in my mouth and then crack my knuckles.

"Officer Joe. You're my backup, man." I slide my gaze over to him and grin. He's all Mr. Serious with his aviators on and arms folded over his chest. His badass gun sits tucked in the back of his slacks. All I get is a simple nod in response.

"Suzy Q," I holler out. "Bring it on."

Aunt Suzy comes sauntering up wearing a cheerleader outfit, a giant smile plastered on her bright purple lips and her signature scarf tied neatly around her head. Presley and Agatha both giggle at her silly outfit. I wink at her. Bones has bitches.

"I beg your pardon, Bones!" Agatha gasps.

I flash Presley an "oh shit" look before storming off into the darkness. Where I know Kady is hiding. Where soon she'll run back to Yeo and dump Kenneth's destructive ass back where it belongs. Where we'll end those assholes once and for all.

"Ready Po-Po Pig?" I ask Officer Joe.

He grunts but draws his gun. In our world, his gun doesn't do shit but he feels good carrying the damn thing around. Whatever floats his police boat.

"How much longer?"

I shrug my shoulders at him and tap my foot on the

ground.

Music.

We need music.

"Yo, Suzy Q!" I holler, my voice echoing around in the darkness. "We need some fight music."

"Ooh," she squeals. "I have just the thing!"

Seconds later, Meghan Trainor's *Lips Are Movin'* thunders around us. Both Officer Joe and I cringe in motherfucking horror. Presley starts dancing and her brown pigtails bounce with her movement. Whiskers, like us dudes, is not amused.

I meet Aunt Suzy's gaze with a raised eyebrow. "Something badass," I clarify.

She huffs and changes the music.

Sabotage by Beastie Boys.

Now we're motherfuckin' talkin'.

All we need now is that douchebag Kenneth.

"Come out, come out, wherever you are!"

While we wait, I pull a joint from my pocket. In Kady's world, I have to use a zippo. In *our* world, I use a badass blowtorch. Officer Joe gives me the side eye as I attempt not to engulf my hair in flames. Once the cherry's lit, I smirk at him.

"The law don't live here," I remind him, a cloud of smoke billowing around from my mouth.

He flips me off. "Just be ready for him."

"Kady!" I holler. "I know you're hiding. I'm not gonna ask nicely, baby girl. Get the fuck outta here and back out there with your man!"

Agatha huffs from behind me. "Language, Bones

Marshall!"

More giggles from my girl Presley. And a terribly annoyed meow from the cat.

"Sorry," I say and shrug my shoulders, muttering under my breath. "Not really sorry."

"I heard that," she grumbles.

I'm chuckling when things go blissfully calm. The calm means happy. Happy means Yeo. *Good girl.*

But the moment I sense she's gone, I feel it.

I feel him.

The self-hatred. The loathing. The motherfucking sadness. It sucks the damn life right out of my chest. I let out a groan.

"Time to go, buddy," I snarl as I charge for Kenneth.

He's hiding in the shadows. The shadows are where his friends Norman and Pascale hide too. We all hate the fucking shadows. The normal members of our unusual family.

But these guys?

They're not family.

They're evil.

Dark and twisted.

Those fuckers live to destroy.

Well...not on my watch.

I stomp off toward him, my size thirteen combat boots echoing in the darkness. You know what they say about shoe size? Yeah, I've got a big dick. But that's a story for a later date...

"Where the hell is he?" Officer Joe hisses.

Poor guy hates the shadows too. But right now, it's a matter of survival. And those things that live in them end now.

Sadness.

Thick and suffocating surrounds me.

We're close.

So fucking close.

And then I hear it.

Kenneth's heavy breathing. Choppy and rushed. He's afraid. Well he should be goddamned afraid. He hurt our girl. So many times he hurt Kadence. So many times I was incapable of stopping him. I wasn't able to do it alone.

But we have Yeo.

He makes Kady strong.

He helps her fight on the outside.

And we wage war on the inside.

"Say goodbye, Crazy Kenny."

The first punch I land on him resounds with a sickening pop.

Over and over again.

Officer Joe doesn't try to arrest him or send him away.

Kenny always comes back.

This time, Officer Joe lets me do what I've been trying to do since the day he showed up when Kady was just a teenager.

I kill the motherfucker.

And he ain't comin' back.

chapter twenty

Yeo

Her entire body is drenched in sweat. The blood from her thighs soaks the comforter and my clothes. As soon as she lets out a relieved sob in my arms, I relax my grip on her.

"There you are, Kadydid," I coo against her damp hair. I press a kiss against her head and lift up.

"It hurts." Tears well and then trickle down the side of her temples as she looks up at me. "Why does he always hurt me?"

I run my palm along the side of her pretty face. God, if I could take away every ounce of pain—physical and mental—I'd do it in a heartbeat. If only it were that easy.

"He's not going to hurt you anymore," I vow, my eyes narrowing.

Her bloody hand flutters over her bare chest and she presses her fingertips into the flesh above her heart. "I ache." Teary blue eyes that look like mini lakes flash to mine. "Here."

Sliding my hand over hers, I look down at her and smile. "Because you miss your mom?"

She grits her teeth and her eyes dart back and forth. I recognize the panicked look. The look she sometimes gets when she doesn't want to discuss the hard stuff and she bails. Mentally. Just checks the fuck out.

Not today.

"Kadydid..."

Guilt flashes in her eyes and her bottom lip wobbles. "I miss her so much. It was my fault you know."

A swell of anger blooms in my chest. Fucking Norman and the stupid lies he tells her.

"It was not your fault," I growl.

She sniffles and casts her gaze to the ceiling as if to remember. "He came for me. He wanted to see me. All he wanted was for me to spend weekends with him. If Mommy would have let him, she'd still be alive."

I close my eyes and will away the fury surging through me. When my eyes reopen, I affix her with a firm glare. "Your father was a sick man. She was protecting you. If you'd gone off with him, he'd have done horrible things to you."

A shudder ripples through her. I know it's from the thought of Norman but it jars me back to the present. She needs medical attention.

"Come on," I say sliding out of the bed and pulling her with me. "Let's get you cleaned up so I can take a look at your legs."

Her knees wobble and she falls against my chest. I kiss

her head once more before leaving the bedroom that holds awful memories with her tucked firmly against my side.

"We're going to get through this," I assure her.

"I sure hope so."

It's been several weeks since the incident. Since that bastard carved what I later learned was a word. *Pain.* He sliced up my Kady like she was a fucking pumpkin. Thankfully, it wasn't deep enough to require stitches. And the fact that he's not coming back—not ever—has me feeling better about the entire situation.

Bones followed through.

Instead of simply running Kenneth off like he's done in the past, he ended him. I'm not really sure what he did. With Bones, you never know. He'd bragged about machine guns and a bloodbath and bitches begging for his nuts. Something tells me it was simpler. Either way, I'm glad Kenneth is gone.

One down, two to go.

"What if he hates me?" Kady murmurs.

I look up from my computer and frown. Today she's a picture of sweet perfection. She's donning a loose-fitting strappy white summer dress with pale pink flowers and has pulled her hair into a sleek ponytail. Her cheeks are slightly rosy still from our lovemaking session in her bed this morning. Just remembering how she called my name over and over again as I made her feel how much I love her has my dick thickening in response.

Snapping my laptop closed, I stand and make my way over to her. We've recently moved into the building Dad paid cash for. It's not gigantic, but it suits the needs for Anderson Counseling and Psychotherapy. The furniture has long since been delivered, but there's still so much to do before we're ready to open.

"Kush?" I sneak a peek at the clock. He should be here any time.

She nods and rests her cheek to my chest once I pull her into my arms. "I'm crazy."

I let out a chuckle at her hissed words. "You're not crazy."

"You know what I mean," she says with a sigh. "Messed up. He's your friend and I may do something to scare him away."

Gripping her hair, I tug it back so I can look into her blue eyes that flicker with sadness. "Kush is a good guy. Not only is he friendly and easygoing, but he also graduated at the top of our class. He's the smartest man, aside from my father, I know. There's nothing going on with you that he hasn't already seen or dealt with on a much greater scale. The rounds we did in the psych ward would make your skin crawl, Kadydid." I don't tell her she's actually the most extreme case I've ever studied. "Plus, you're beautiful and sweet. I may have to beat him off with a stick."

She giggles and I wink at her.

"Well, well, well," a familiar voice says from the doorway, sounding exactly like Mr. Smith from *The Matrix*. "Mr. Anderson."

"My name is Neo," I tell him through gritted teeth, just

like the character from the movie. Our nerdism for those movies is ultimately what made us become friends.

We both chuckle. I release Kady and stride over to Kush. He wears a half grin on his dark skin as he admires my office. His quirky style hasn't changed. He wears a pale purple plaid suit and a black vest underneath. Kush is a tie freak and never leaves home without one. Today's tie is dark purple and sleek. The black hair on his head is standing up in every direction and his thick eyebrows are quirked up as he skims over the view of my office—the only room in the building that's fully decorated.

"How you been, buddy?" I question as I shake his hand before pulling him into a hug.

He pats my shoulder. "Better now that I'm here."

I pull away and gesture toward the most beautiful girl on the planet. Her unease is evident. She twists her fingers together and nervously shifts her balance from one leg to the other. With her head bowed and looking at the rug, I can't make out her features.

Stay with me, Kady.

"Kush, meet my girl, Kadence Marshall," I say, pride in my tone.

Her chin lifts and she flashes me a small smile. There's no doubt I love this girl. It still blows my mind she has trouble believing it sometimes.

"Kady, meet my friend, Kush Pawan."

Kush saunters over to her and offers not only his hand but one of his signature grins that used to get him his fair share of chicks back in college. Thankfully, Kady is immediately disarmed. A slight blush creeps up her cheeks and she offers her hand.

"Lovely to meet you," he tells her genuinely. "Yeo has told me so much about you."

And I have. He's one of the few people who knows everything. After a long, drunken night of despairing over Kady hiding and fucking Bones in her place, I spilled to Kush. Ever the doctor, he began picking apart my brain for answers. Like me, he wanted to understand her. He never once told me I should move on or get past her.

"Oh," Kady says, her voice dropping to a whisper. "I'm sorry."

Kush raises an eyebrow at her. "Sorry for what? The kid's in love with you. He used to gush about you so much. Hell, even I had a crush on you."

I laugh and shake my head.

Kady's eyes flicker to mine in confusion before sliding back to Kush. "He told you about…about my…"

"Your nine alters. Yes."

She chews on her bottom lip. "They make life difficult sometimes," she admits. "I don't have much control over who shows up."

Kush nods thoughtfully. He steps away from her and walks over to my bookcase which is now lined with my medical books. I draw her back to my side to hug her tight. She's not as tense as I'd have expected. Kady doesn't normally do well with new people, but here she is. Still in my arms. Still Kady. Every day is progress with her.

"I once read about a patient who had over a hundred alters," he tells her. He looks over his shoulder and regards her. "Do yours work as a family?"

He knows this but I let him try to get to know her in his own way. The Kush way. He's good at making people feel comfortable and not on the spot. People open up to him freely. They aren't intimidated by the nerdy dressing dude.

"Yeah. There are a few who simply live to wreak havoc though." Her voice is a whisper. Anger wells inside of me. Just the idea of having Pascale and Norman on the loose is enough to have my blood boiling. And this is why I need Kush. She needs psychotherapy but it has to be with someone I trust. But it also can't be me. I'm too involved and partial to her afflictions. We need someone who's heart isn't also in the fray.

"Do they make appearances often?" His eyes meet hers for a moment before he's strolling over to my desk to fuck with shit over there too. He picks up one of my pens and starts clicking at it while he waits for her to answer.

"Pascale hides when Yeo is around. He hates Yeo." She looks up and beams at me. As if I'm her damn hero. My heart soars from that smile much like it did when I was ten years old and told her I loved her cat Whiskers. Back then I was her hero too. "And Norman..." Her smile falls as her eyes grow distant.

"Who is Norman?" Kush's voice is just deep and commanding enough that it drags her from her mental retreat.

She shudders but turns her attention his way. "My dad."

"Where's your real dad?"

Her shoulders hunch and she swallows loudly. "Prison."

The tension is thick, but I don't dare interrupt their moment. Sensing that she's teetering, Kush backs off.

"You like pizza, Miss Kady?"

Thrown off by his question, she snaps her gaze to mine. I shrug my shoulders and smile.

"Um, yeah. Why?"

He pats his belly and saunters over to the window. "That place across the street is calling my name. All I've had for the past month is my mom's home cooked Indian food. And while I appreciate a good meal, a man must have pizza every now and again. I'm long overdue."

Kush holds out a hand to her. She hesitates for a moment but then accepts his offer. Then, my girl walks off with her doctor.

My heart roars with happiness.

And my mind whispers.

Everything will be okay now.

I'll give it to Kush. The man can roll with the punches. Right now, as we wait for our pizzas to arrive, he's holding his own with none other than Aunt Suzy.

"Fourteen," she reminds him, batting her eyelashes in a flirtatious way. "Fourteen cases of bottled water at the Two Dollar Store for just three seventy-four. Can you believe it?"

He sips at his iced tea and then lets out a whistle. "Miss Suzy, I must say that is quite a deal. Coupon cutting was a fad, I thought. But here you are still saving your family lots of money. That's admirable."

Aunt Suzy beams and then mouths blatantly at me. *Oh, I like him.*

I smirk and nod before mouthing back. *I like him too.*

She straightens her back and then leans forward as if to hang onto every word he says. He surprises both of us when he cuts to the chase.

"Miss Suzy," he questions, his voice growing serious. "Where's Kady?"

Her smile falls and she purses her lips together. "That girl is a master at hide-and-seek. When things get tough, she lets us do the heavy lifting."

Kush narrows his eyes. "I see. But why would she run from me? I thought she liked me."

Guilt flashes in Aunt Suzy's eyes. She swallows thickly and gives him a false smile. "She does. I'm not sure why she's hiding, to be quite honest."

He reaches across the table and pats her hand. "Can you bring her back to me?"

Aunt Suzy is always so flamboyant and happy. The fact that she seems uncomfortable has my hackles slightly raised. My hands curl into fists. I'm protective over all of them.

"Calm down, lover boy," Kush says, making eye contact with me. "Just want to talk to Miss Kady." With his eyes he implores me to let him do his thing. I let out a rush of breath and give him a clipped nod.

"I'll see what I can do," Aunt Suzy tells him.

A moment later, she turns her head to look at me. Kady's bright blue eyes flicker with confusion. That one brief second when she comes back to reality is always frightening for her. But she locates my comforting gaze and relaxes.

"I'm so sorry," she squeaks out and leans into my side.

I pull her against me and rub up and down her arm.

"Why are you sorry, beautiful?"

Her head turns and she meets Kush's interested stare. "Are you, um, mad?"

Kush lets out a loud, boisterous laugh that makes half the restaurant flick their attention over to us. "Of course I'm not mad. I just wanted to talk to *you*."

She relaxes when he launches into how his sister also plays piano. Kady perks up and carries on a very animated conversation with him about music. Her happiness seems to saturate every soul in her proximity. I love when Kady is…Kady. No past. No stress. No fear. Simply Kady. Talking about what she loves. Smiling. Laughing. Enjoying *her* life.

Not theirs.

Hers.

Our food comes and we eat as three friends. So normal. No family interruptions. No Norman outbursts. Just us.

Don't worry, Kady. Kush and I will help you get your life back.

For the first time in so long, hope begins to warm my heart. I hope that we can begin to free Kady from some of the chains that weigh her down.

The girl was meant to soar…

Eventually, we're going to break her loose and give her the freedom she deserves.

chapter twenty-one

Kady

"Tell me about how you met each alter," Kush says, scratching at the scruff along his jaw that's recently grown in. "I want to know how each one was born."

Disgust washes over me and I cringe. Before Bones came along, I'd been a part of some terrible things with my father. So terrible that I've shoved them far into the recesses of my mind. I hope to never explore them ever again. I don't ever want to remember those times with him and me alone in my bedroom.

"Kady," he implores, leaning forward in his leather seat. He places his elbows on his knees and maintains eye contact with me.

I chew on my lip and dart my gaze over to the clock on the wall. Thirty minutes. I'd promised Yeo I would sit with Kush three times a week for thirty minutes. We're only four minutes in and I'm ready to bolt. "Um," I start, my voice hoarse and scratchy, "Bones came when I was tired of my father hurting me. I'd been craving to hurt my daddy back."

His lips purse together and his kind eyes look sad. He feels sorry for me. Kush's obvious emotion makes me uncomfortable.

"Did you understand who this Bones was?" he questions with furrowed brows.

"Not entirely. At least not at first."

I fidget in my seat and check the time again. Twenty-five minutes to go.

"When were you aware that he wasn't real?"

His words cause me to flinch. "He's real…" My heart thunders in my chest. "To me, he's real."

Kush picks up his mug from the table and takes a sip of the hot coffee that I know the new receptionist, Amber, made. He and Yeo have been here for three weeks now and they've begun to see some patients. Amber is quiet but nice. She's what some would consider overweight but she's by far the prettiest woman I've ever seen. Her light brown hair hangs in waves around her face and her bright green eyes twinkle with happiness. Always. What I wouldn't give to have that twinkle in my own eyes.

But I am happy…

Ever since Yeo came back, life has been simpler.

He takes care of me in every sense of the word. We rarely spend any time apart because I think he's afraid he'll lose me again. My family has grown quiet, aside from Bones, and the dark men who haunt me seem to be hanging out off my radar. Life is actually good. Normal even.

"So who came next?" Kush questions, dragging me from my inner thoughts.

A smile tugs at my lips. "Whiskers. I'd always wanted a pet but was never allowed one. Then, one day after crying my eyes out, Bones told me about Whiskers. I like cats." A pleased sigh escapes me.

Kush smiles. He likes cats too. "Sounds lovely. But your cat is a non-human alter. Right?"

My lips tug down into a frown. In my head, it all seems so real. Yeo and I created the book to help us both understand my mind a little better. But I've never been forced to discuss in great lengths about each one. Never have I had to determine their origins or face the fact that they aren't actually living, breathing beings but instead slivers of my psyche formed when it cracked and splintered because of all the mental anguish I'd been through over my twenty-nine years of life.

"He's an alter, yes," I admit.

Fear trickles through me. Fear of dissecting each part of me. I'm afraid that when I drag them all into the light and under a microscope, they'll lose their powers. That they'll disappear and I'll be all alone. All alone and forced to deal with life by myself.

"Is this upsetting you, Kady? Am I making you feel uncomfortable?"

My eyes flip up to his and I attempt a smile but it falls flat. "Kind of. Yeo knows about them, and now so does his family, but we've never outright discussed all of it."

Kush tugs at the knot on his tie to loosen it just a bit. His voice is low and gravelly. "Why didn't your grandma ever take you to counseling?"

The mention of my grandma causes an ache to cut

through me like a dull knife. She passed away when I was eighteen. I'd been devastated.

"She said they wouldn't understand me. That they'd medicate me and take me away from her. Grandma was so sad after my mother died," I tell him absently. I remember the way I'd catch Grandma staring out the window as if she'd magically see her daughter come bouncing up the front porch. It never happened.

"Your grandma loved you very much," he tells me. "She was protecting you. Just like Yeo protects you. And just like your alters protect you."

I smile. Yeo is so fierce when it comes to me. He's been that way since we first met. Always caring about my wellbeing.

"But," Kush says, his tone serious. "I'm not here to protect you."

My entire body tenses and I snap my gaze to his. "W-What?"

His words are firm but he says them in a kind way. "I'm not here to protect you. I'm here to help you. Helping you means talking through the memories you have repressed. Helping you is discussing your alters and finding ways to live life without their help. Helping you means encouraging you to face your fears instead of hiding from them. I'm here to help, Kadence Marshall."

The clock on the wall says I still have twenty-one minutes with him. Twenty-one long minutes. I'm not sure I can take that many minutes of cutting open my mind and spilling the contents for him to play around in. That awful part of me is locked up for a reason. Hidden because I can't bear for it to be free.

"Kady…"

Kady. Kady. Kady.

I'm scared.

Black. Black. Black.

"We need to call the police, Louise. They've been looking for him since we filed the report last week," Grandma says, her wrinkled lips pursing together with worry. "He's violent and crazy and needs to be put away. And now he's calling all of the time threatening you. When will this end?"

Mommy's lip trembles and a tear streaks down her cheek. Her nose is dark purple and still swollen. Whenever she talks, it reminds me of the time she had the flu because she sounds stopped up.

"That's exactly why we can't call them. They won't do anything and then he'll retaliate." Mommy's eyes won't meet mine. "He said…I just can't call them, okay?"

I drop my gaze to my lap. Dark bruises paint my fair skin. Bruises Daddy put there. A shudder ripples through me. Bones won't tell me what Daddy did to him. In fact, he hasn't spoken to me at all. I can sense whatever it was happened to be very painful.

"I'm getting a gun," Grandma states, fury making her voice rise a few octaves. "I'll shoot that bastard if he touches one hair on either of my girls' heads ever again." Her tone softens and she gives me a regretful stare. "I wish one of you would've woken me up. You know that CPAP machine makes

it impossible to hear outside my bedroom door. If only I'd have known he'd come into the house, I could have stopped..."

Both her and Mommy look over at me.

I'm panicking under their intense stare when I hear Bones. Finally.

"She couldn't have stopped him," he tells me simply. "He's a mean fucker. There's no telling what he would have done to your grandma."

Tears well in my eyes and I nod. Daddy might have hit Grandma too. And she's too old to endure what Daddy does to me and Mommy.

"I'm fine, Kady," he assures me. His voice is a whisper. I love it when he whispers. "Besides, who else is going to protect you from that monster? Badass Bones is who. Stop your worrying, silly."

The tight ache in my chest loosens and I let out a sigh. Grandma and Mommy talk lowly to one another but I'm no longer focused on them. I focus on Bones.

Bones will protect me.

He always does.

Bones

This nerdy motherfucker is looking at me like I've got the goddamned plague. I want to tell him he's poisoning *me* with his dumbass outfit. Who the fuck wears plaid anymore? I feel like I've been dumped onto the set of *Three's Company.* Oh, God, what I wouldn't give to fuck the 80s right out of Chrissy. I would make her wear those sexy-as-fuck leg warmers and—

"Who are you?"

Nerd Boy narrows his gaze at me and plucks me right from my fantasy. It was just getting to the good part too.

"I'm Kady and Kitty Muncher's best friend. Motherfuckin' Bones. Who the fuck are you?" I demand.

His eyes widen for a moment but then he steels his gaze at me. "Did Kady send you?"

"Are we answering questions with questions now?" I throw back at him.

"Are you always this difficult?

I scoff. "Are you always the worst dressed idiot in the room?"

His lip curls up. "Do you always walk around with no shirt on?"

"Do you want to suck my cock?"

"Does Yeo know his name is tattooed on your chest?"

I narrow my eyes at him. "Does your momma know you're a little bitch?"

He reaches over and tosses a dress at me.

The fabric smells like Kady. I sling it back at him. "Do I look like a fuckin' chick to you?"

Nerd Boy shrugs out of his jacket and throws it into my lap. "Will you please put this on?"

Her dress is more preferable to the plaid abomination in my grip. "Do you always dress like your grandpa?"

His eyes close and he takes a deep breath but doesn't reopen them. "Let's try this again. I'm Dr. Pawan. You may call me Kush if that makes you feel more comfortable."

I blink at him. With a roll of my eyes, I let his jacket slide to the floor and I lean back against the cool leather. After I prop my feet up on the coffee table, I cross my arms and lift an eyebrow at him. "Okay, Dr. Dweeb," I tell him with a grunt. "Why the fuck did you scare my girl?"

He shoots me an exasperated look before quickly closing his eyes again. "I thought she was Yeo's girl."

Just the mention of Yeo's name has my heart beating out of my goddamned chest. It's been weeks since I've seen him. Kady just seems so...happy. I hate barging in on her shit. As much as I want to see Kitty Muncher and have his cock buried in my ass, I simply can't. I can't push my way through to see him when she's enjoying her time with him. I would never do that to her.

"Yeah, so?" I admit with a huff.

"But you love and care for her?"

Anger swells inside of me. "What kind of stupid ass question is that, Dr. Dweeb? Of course I fucking love her. She's my best friend."

He runs his fingers through his bushy hair. I think I rile him up for some reason. "I'm glad she has people who care for her. But..." His head turns toward me and his dark eyes pin me. "You're not actually a person."

My nose flares at his words. Fury surges through my veins and I fist my hands. *Keep talking, asshole. Keep talking.* "Are you trying to get my size thirteen foot rammed up your ass?"

His gaze falls to my feet. I frown when I look down and see pink toenail polish. Fucking Presley and her girly shit.

"Those look to be about a size seven, if you ask me," he

says in a bland tone.

I wiggle my toes. If I didn't think it'd upset that little girl, I'd take a black sharpie to them. "Whatever. At least I know why Kady asked me to come deal with you. You're annoying as fuck."

Dr. Dweeb shakes his head. "She felt threatened, yes. I asked her about each of her alters, including you. I asked her to describe how they were born. Do you understand that you are, in fact, an alter? That you're just a splintered part of her personality attempting to preserve and protect her mind."

"You're speaking gobbly-goo, dude. I don't know what the fuck you're talking about."

He smiles and it annoys me. "Yeo tells me you all know about the book. That you helped him create it. You're all aware that you're simply a part of her. Nothing more."

I shrug. I'm three seconds from walking the fuck out of here.

"I want to work with her on how to deal with stress and anxiety on her own. My goal is to coach her through certain moments. I hope that she could learn to deal with them by herself and not call for her alters when she feels her control slipping."

His face is genuine and guilt begins trickling its way through me. I know Yeo asked her to have therapy sessions with this dipshit. He wants her to get better. Now that Kenneth's gone and the other two have been hiding, she actually has a chance at some normalcy.

"You're the doctor," I tell him, my tone flippant. "Not me. Do your doctory shit and leave me out of it."

His lips tug down and he looks sad. "That's exactly what I'd like to do. Leave you out of it. To leave all of her alters out of it."

Uneasiness washes over me. "What exactly are you saying?"

"Clearly, Bones, you're the strongest of all her alters. The first and the one she loves the most. You have the power to tell her no. To make the others tell her no."

The very idea of Kady calling for one of us and us ignoring her makes me want to throw the fuck up. Dr. Dweeb probably wouldn't like Cheetos vomit all over his fancy rug. That shit would stain.

"Not gonna happen. When Kady needs me, I help her. End of."

Except that one time…but that'll never happen again.

"These are things she can handle."

I close my eyes. Norman's terrifying face glares back at me. "She couldn't handle *him*," I hiss. "*I* could barely fucking handle him."

"Who?"

"NORMAN!" I roar, my chest heaving with angry breaths.

"What did Norman do? What happened?"

I drag my fingers through my wild dark hair and let out a groan. My eyes remain pinched shut. I hate the things he did. They're forever burned into my head. I work daily trying to cut them the fuck out of my mind.

"What did Norman do?" he implores.

"EVERYTHING! He did fucking everything! No child should ever have to go through that shit," I snarl. "He was sick. So goddamned sick!"

The room grows quiet and I reopen my eyes. Dr. Dweeb's eyes are pained as he regards me with sadness.

"I'm sorry you had to endure that, Bones."

I swallow and shrug my shoulders. "Whatever. It is what it is. Better me than her."

"You were just a kid, too. You shouldn't have had to be the recipient of his physical and sexual abuse."

My head begins to throb. With the butt of my hand, I pound into my forehead. On occasion, I get these fucked up migraines. They're brought on when I'm stressed. And when I'm like this, I struggle with my ability to assist Kady. I fade out into oblivion.

"Bones." His words are concerned but are quickly turning into whispers.

I like whispers…

Bones. Bones. Bones.

"Bones!"

I LOVE ROARS…

My normal strength begins to weaken. And that only means one thing.

"Dr. Dweeb," I mutter through clenched teeth as the room spins. "Go get Kitty Muncher. It's important. Tell him…" I pound at my forehead to drive away the madness. "T-Tell him *he's* not packin' but he's a comin' and it ain't gonna be pretty."

chapter twenty-two

Yeo

"I knew this was a bad idea," I grumble as I cruise down the street looking for Pascale. As soon as Kush barged into my office with horror twisting his features, I knew something had happened. Not just something but someone. By the time we made it back to his office though, Pascale was gone.

The very idea of him traipsing around town in nothing but Kush's blazer has me sick to my stomach. When Kush told me about Bones's appearance, I'd felt an ache in my chest. Bones has been laying low lately. And while I enjoy spending more time with Kady, I do miss Bones.

"It wasn't a bad idea, Yeo," Kush assures me. "This is the only way to help her. If I can learn about her alters and then get them to acknowledge exactly what they are, I believe I can at least urge them to do what's best for Kady. Bones does seem to care about her. I think he'll do what needs to be done to help. But…"

"Her bad alters are still a fucking problem. Yes, I know this." I shake my head and turn down a road that leads toward one of Pascale's favorite hangouts. "We already got rid of one of them. The other two are worse, though. Stronger and more destructive. It's a process."

He starts to say something but my phone rings. Absently, I answer without checking to see who it is.

"Duuuuude," Barclay says before I even mutter a hello.

"What? I don't have time for this shit right now, man," I snap. The tension in my neck becomes a painful throb. "What do you want?"

He huffs like he's running and I almost laugh. The very idea of Barclay running anywhere but after Dad is comical. He's always too busy trying to get everyone's attention. To show them how much of a badass he is by *running* his mouth. Never does he do anything remotely physical.

"I, uh, Jesus I need to get back to the gym," he grunts. "I saw, uh, her. Actually, I, uh…"

"Spit it the fuck out, Barc," I seethe.

"What's the thug one? Um, your girlfriend…"

I roll my eyes. "Pascale?"

"Yeah, so I'm driving to the hotel to go over some possible design elements they wanted to add and I see this half-naked chick running down the road. Fuck, ow!" He howls and then lets out another grunt.

"What the hell is happening?" I demand. I glance over at Kush and shake my head in frustration. Putting the phone on speaker, I toss it on the dash and turn down a road that will take me to another of Pascale's places.

"Shit, I think I rolled my ankle. I can't run in dress

shoes, dammit. Anyway, so I recognize the chick as Kady but she's wearing some old man's blazer. I'm talking 1983 and shit…" Another grunt. "Get out of the way!" More shuffling. "Anyway, so I'm all like stunned by this ugly ass jacket"—Kush grumbles and shakes his head, clearly annoyed because it's his jacket—"and then I'm all like, Yeo's chick is makin' a dude face. Looking all kinds of grumpy and not like Kady. So I remembered what you'd said and I think it's the punk personality."

"Alter," both Kush and I groan at the same time.

"Whatever. So, I jump out of my car and chase after her. Him. Whatever the fuck I'm supposed to call it and—"

"Address, Barc."

He rattles off the road he's running down and I haul ass in that direction. I'm getting closer when I hear a bunch of commotion on Barc's end of the phone.

Grunting.

Snarling.

Cursing.

I gas it and when I round the corner, I see my brother. He's looking proud as punch as he holds my half-naked girl in his arms. God, how she squirms. Barc's lucky Pascale didn't come from home. He'd have knifed his ass or something. But since Pascale left straight from the practice, he'd been limited to Kady's panties and Kush's jacket.

"Pascale seems like a nightmare," Kush mutters as I whip my car over to the side of the road.

"You have no idea."

I bolt from the car and charge over to them. Barc has a death grip around Pascale from behind. When I near,

Pascale has the sense to look afraid.

"Fuckin' stalker," he hisses and attempts to spit at me.

I grip his jaw and get in his face. I'm careful not to bite into his flesh too hard because Kady will be the one to suffer. Not this asshole. "LEAVE!" I growl. "LEAVE HER THE FUCK ALONE!"

He struggles but Barc's grip tightens. Pascale lets out a string of curse words.

"Are you Pascale?" Kush utters from behind me.

Pascale narrows his eyes at him. "Fuck you."

Kush lets out a sigh and approaches him from beside me. He nudges me and I reluctantly drop my grip from Pascale's jaw. "You're a figment of Kady's mind, Pascale. You're not welcome here. Everything you are is toxic. You have no purpose."

Pascale glares at him but then confusion sets in. "What are you? The fuckin' Oracle?"

Kush lets out a laugh. "Pascale, have you ever even seen that movie? Do you know the title?"

The alter blinks at Kush as if he's the one who's lost his mind.

With a rush of breath, Kush continues on quickly. "Kady's seen that movie plenty of times with Yeo. I know this because he's told me every detail about Kady. You know about the Oracle because Kady's seen *The Matrix*. Not you. You're tapping into Kady's memories. You're nothing but a bad part of her personality. You are absolutely nothing without her."

Pascale shakes his head. "You pricks are fuckin' loco."

Kush squats down on the ground and Pascale's gaze

follows him. "Pink toes? What kind of gangster has pink toes?"

Barc snorts with laughter. "They got you, man."

"No…" Pascale utters. He's no longer struggling in my brother's arms. "No."

"Yes," Kush says firmly as he stands. "Now give us Kady back."

She's been sleeping ever since Pascale left her. Surprisingly, upon learning about what he really is, Pascale bailed. I'd wanted to draw Bones out and beg for him to finish Pascale off but Kady simply passed out. Barc surprised me when he followed Kush and I back to Kady's house. He'd been oddly supportive. My brother actually helped when it came to Kady. Barclay didn't hesitate or make fun of her—he simply chased after her. Once we'd settled her in her bed, the three of us openly discussed what had happened. Barc had some questions. Kush had some answers. I mostly just floated by wondering how the fuck to get the bad ones in her head to leave her alone.

Now that they're gone, I've been curled up against her in her bed. While asleep, she looks like an innocent angel without a care in the world. I love to see her so carefree.

"Does Kady know you're a fucking creeper, Kitty Muncher?"

My heart jolts to life in my chest and I gaze right into Bones's sad eyes. "Where've you been, man?" I can't help the accusatory tone in my voice. I know that Kush says that we're trying to push them away and in the process draw her out, but I don't think as clearly when it comes to Bones and Kady.

His lips twitch like he might smile but he doesn't. Instead, he brings a shaky palm to my cheek. "Why do you have to look so goddamned good?"

I crack a smile and press a kiss to his soft lips. "Because I like driving you crazy."

His fingers spear into my hair. He clutches me like I might vanish into thin air. "I'm already crazy, Yeo. Don't need you stirring the pot and adding shit to make it extra fucked up." His mouth opens to grant me access. I graze my tongue along his bottom lip before darting it between his lips. Our kiss is needy but not rushed. Desperate but not frantic. God, I've missed him.

"Where have you been?" I demand and pull back to glare at him, anger washing over me. "I've been wondering if you're okay, asshole. You like playing hide-and-seek like Kady too? Do you two know how fucking much that hurts me?"

His eyes tear from mine. I grip his jaw and jerk him back to me. Our lips meet again. This time our kiss is angry. He nips at my lip and I devour him. I've just begun kissing along his cheek toward his throat when he let's out a strangled sound.

I lift up and peer down at him.

"I'm not so strong anymore," he admits, his voice cracking with emotion. "God, how I've wanted to see you. To let you fuck me. To just smell you, goddammit. But..." His eyes become bloodshot with unshed tears. "I can't do that to her. She's so fucking happy with you."

I run my nose along his and pepper kisses all over his beautiful face. "But I miss you."

He lets out a pained sounding chuckle. "I can't take her away from you. I'm not selfish like that. Since you've been back, I can feel her growing stronger each day. You're so fucking good for her, man. She needs you."

I hug him to me and bury my face in his long hair. "She and I both need you, Bones. Hiding isn't helping anyone except letting assholes like Pascale slip by."

His body grows tense in my arms. I lift up to regard his expression. Dark brows are furled and his face is murderous. "He won't be slipping by ever again."

"Did you…"

I won't allow myself to hope.

"I got rid of him. Just like I got rid of Kenneth." His gaze is sad. This time he isn't bragging of machine guns and bitches. He doesn't regale me on how Guns N' Roses played live background music to his epic showdown.

No…

A tear slips out.

And with it, my heart slides right out with it, crashing to the floor.

"This was the plan," I whisper.

Bones likes whispers. He's told me so.

"The plan is exhausting," he admits. "The plan is taking its toll."

I frown, unable to understand what he means. "All we have left is Norman. Get rid of him and Kady will be free."

Bones swallows and looks off toward the window. "I

don't think I have the strength to do it again. Especially not with him…" His eyes close and he shudders. "I fucking hate him so goddamned much."

"Shh," I murmur and begin pressing more kisses to his flesh. "Don't worry about that crap right now. We'll get rid of him eventually. I swear."

"He's too strong," he chokes out. "It's not that easy."

"But you're stronger," I growl, my voice a quiet roar.

Bones loves roars. He's told me so.

I kiss him until it grows dark outside.

I touch him all over in an effort to memorize every surface of him.

I love his body through the night, every single thrust a display of my affection.

Kady doesn't come back for the rest of the night.

And just this one time, I don't beg her to.

chapter twenty-three

Kady

I stare at my reflection in my dresser mirror. The white lacey dress I'm wearing fits my body well. Over the past couple of months, I've gained some weight and the color has returned to my cheeks.

Yeo nourishes me.

Body and soul.

But especially my emaciated mind.

It's been a couple of weeks since Pascale disappeared for good. Just like when Kenneth had gone, I felt a loss inside me. Both of them would hurt me in their own ways and yet I still ached where they left a hole inside. I never verbalized this to Yeo or Kush. They'd only think I was more crazy than I already was.

Despite being happy that Yeo is by my side twenty-four-seven like old times, I still can't help but feel sort of confused. It's weird to go to Walmart. Normally Aunt Suzy does the shopping but now that Yeo's here, he insists we do it together. And we do. With his hand gripping mine, I'm able to ignore people's stares. I'm able to help him pick out food without any real meltdowns.

But Whiskers's toys are left in the same place he discarded them weeks ago.

Presley hasn't picked up her coloring books in I don't know how long.

Officer Joe doesn't bring by peanut butter and bread anymore.

The house is getting dusty. Agatha would have a fit. Except she doesn't.

And Bones...

That big mouth is so quiet.

The pantry full of Cheetos remains full. No notes written on paper towels. No black T-shirts strung out all over the house. No whispers.

"Bones," I murmur. "Are you mad at me?"

I close my eyes and seek out his warmth. Just when I think I may feel it wrapping around me from behind, it is instantly snuffed out with the sound of Yeo's voice.

"You ready?" he questions, his deep voice rattling me to my core.

Our gazes meet in the mirror and his is hungry. A smile tugs at my lips. Yeo is the best thing that's ever happened to me. "I hope they eat our food. It's certainly nothing like Agatha's."

He flashes me a grin before kissing the top of my head. "They'll eat it and they'll be happy. Besides, I already snuck a bite. The pork chops are good, beautiful. Guess you may have been paying more attention to her cooking than you ever realized."

I twist in his arms and kiss his lips tenderly. When I pull away, I regard him with a serious expression. "Do you miss Bones?"

His eyes darken and his jaw clenches. "Yeah."

"Why are they all so quiet?"

"I don't know. Maybe your sessions with Kush are helping," he suggests. I don't miss the sadness flickering in his eyes.

"Then why does it ache if it's helping. I feel empty and..." Tears prickle at my eyes but I blink them away. "Alone."

His fingers clutch onto my chin and he tilts my head up. "You'll never be alone as long as I have anything to do about it. Got it, Kadydid?"

I chuckle and nod. "How'd I get so lucky to have you?"

He smirks. "I pretty much forced my way into your life when we were kids, remember? You were too young to realize you'd befriended a stalker."

I swat at him, causing him to laugh. "I'm not young now. Maybe I'm onto your stalker ways and maybe I like them ..." Looking over my shoulder, I start to walk off. His eyes narrow and he drags his gaze down my backside. A shiver runs through me when he prowls after me.

"You're definitely all grown up," he agrees in a hot whisper against the back of my head. His erection pokes into me. If we weren't having his parent's and Kush over any moment now, I'd beg him to shove my dress up and fuck me really quick. "I'll stalk you until the day I die."

"I love you, Yeo," I tell him with a sigh. He palms my ass

and then pushes the dress up to my hips.

His teeth nip at my shoulder through my dress. "I love you too, beautiful."

"These pork chops are amazing. Gyeong," Fletcher says to his wife with a friendly smile, "you'll have to get the recipe from Kady."

I blush at his praise and Yeo squeezes my thigh under the table.

"I'm learning Kady's a great cook," Yeo tells his father, the pride in his voice warming me all the way to my toes.

Fletcher nods and gives me a wink. I'm still not used to him being nice to me. Now that he finally knows what I am, he seems to have accepted me.

All eyes are off me when Kush launches into some ideas he had to promote their practice. I take the moment to breathe. I'm sawing at my pork chop when I hear a voice I've not heard in ages.

Run.

I lift my gaze from my food. All eyes are on Kush. None of them notice the way my hand trembles violently.

Run.

Kush's words from our session resound in my head. Just breathe, Kady. Remember, you're in control.

Run.

But the whispers are guiding me to my feet. The whispers have me edging away from the table.

Run.

My legs wobble. Fear has immobilized me. I think it's Bones's voice but I can't be sure.

Run.

Whispers chant the word over and over again inside my head until I want to claw them out.

Run.

I have nowhere to run to and the evil from my past yanks me back so fast I don't even realize what's hit me.

"There's my little girl," Daddy mutters in the dark.

I sit up in my bed and scramble backward until my back hits the wall. My eyes search the black shadows for him. Sometimes I have nightmares about him. Sometimes his voices seem so real. Bones tells me to ignore it.

"Kadence." His large form emerges from the closet and I let out a squeak. It's not a dream. Daddy is back!

"Mommy!" What I'd hoped was a roar is only a whisper.

"Shhh," he growls. "We're going to play a game."

I hate Daddy's games.

"N-No," I tell him boldly.

He storms over to me and snatches my elbow. I'm yanked from the bed into his arms where he hugs me tight.

"Bones!"

Daddy slaps a hand over my mouth. "We're leaving. Be quiet, baby."

I squirm as tears roll out. I don't want to go with Daddy!

He drags me out of my bedroom and down the hallway. When we pass Mommy's doorway, Daddy stops. I attempt to scream despite his hold on my mouth. While not much sound comes out, I do manage to kick the door and it makes a loud thump.

"Kadence?" Mommy murmurs from her bed.

As soon as her lamp light floods her bedroom, her eyes widen in horror. "Norman, what are you doing?"

He stalks into the room toward her with me wiggling in his arms. Mommy lets out a whimper and retreats in the bed. I want her to grab onto me so he won't take me with him. "I'm taking our daughter back home where she belongs."

Mommy sits up on her knees and becomes angry. She hardly ever gets angry with Daddy. I think she's scared of him like I am. "You're not taking her anywhere. Momma!" she calls out for Grandma. "Momma, call the cops!"

His body tenses at her defiance and he throws me into the floor so hard I bonk my head. A pounding inside my brain begins thundering. Where is Bones?!

Crack!

The sound jolts me out of my stupor. When I look up, I see Daddy has his fist raised before he slams it against Mommy's face.

"Nooo!" I scramble to my feet and charge for him. He manages to punch her again before I even get close. "Daddy stop!"

But he won't stop. His hair is messy and he's acting like some wild bear mauling my mother.

"Bones! Grandma!"

"K-Kadence," Mommy stutters. "R-Run..."

Crack!

A sob escapes me but I remember how to work my legs.

I run from the bedroom and down the hall to Grandma's room. When I push through her door, she's already tugging at her CPAP mask and has the light on.

"D-D-Daddy is here and he's hurting Mommy!" I shriek.

Grandma climbs out of the bed and shuffles over to her closet. She pulls a shotgun from the closet. I'm fixated on the way she loads two red shells into the barrel before snapping it closed.

"Call 911 and hide under the bed, Kady," Grandma hisses.

I can still hear Mommy hollering in the other room and I'm frozen in my spot.

"Now, Kadence!"

Jumping at her tone, I hurry to her bedside and dial the operator. I can hear shouts in the other room. My heart physically aches at the thought of Daddy hurting Grandma too.

"Just hurry!" I tell the operator after I prattle off the address. She blabs about staying on the line, but I can't. "I need to help Grandma!"

I toss the phone receiver on the bed and run out of the room toward the screams. When I make it to the doorway, my stomach drops to the floor. Mommy is so bloody. He has her hair twisted in his grip and holds a knife to her throat.

Grandma is crying and the gun wobbles in her hands. She has it aimed at him but he holds Mommy in front of him. If Grandma shot the gun, it would hit Mommy first.

"All I want is my kid, Ruth. That's all I've ever fuckin' wanted. But your daughter stole her from me," he snarls, digging the knife harder into Mommy's skin. She sobs as a thick ribbon of blood trickles down below where he has the blade

pressed against her.

"Leave my family alone and get the hell out of my house, Norman. The cops are on their way," *Grandma snaps at him.*

"Give me Kadence and I'll leave you two bitches alone."

I don't want to go with Daddy.

Betrayal seeps its way into my heart because Bones is hiding from me when I need him most. I know he's still upset over what Daddy did to him last week but I need his help. Please come back, Bones.

"You're going to leave, asshole." *Grandma's voice reminds me of a tiger growling. I can't believe she said a curse word!* "You're nothing but a good for nothing wife beating child molester."

I don't know what a child molester is but I think it has something to do with me since I'm the only child around. Please come back, Bones.

"You and I both know you're not going to shoot, bitch," *Daddy taunts.*

Grandma trembles and even I can sense she's afraid to do it.

"Daddy," *I beg*, "please don't hurt my mommy."

He opens his mouth to speak when we hear sirens in the distance. "Fuck!"

His roar startles me and I nearly pee myself.

"Come on, Kadence," *he growls.* "Time to go."

Time stops.

Like in a superhero movie. Everything freezes. I don't want it to unfreeze either because I feel like something really bad is about to happen.

And just like that, Mommy's cries become gargles.

Red and red and red surge from her throat. Daddy shoves her to the floor in front of him. A loud bang resounds in the bedroom. I know he lets out a grunt but it sounds like the wall took most of the bullet spray. I'm not focused on them though.

No.

I have to be the nurse for Mommy. Just like old times. Old times when I would help her get better. Her eyes are halfway shut and her face is pale. I use both of my small hands to hold her wound closed. The blood seeps between my fingers with every passing moment. Behind me, Grandma and Daddy are fighting. I can hear things slamming. Glass shatters. Furniture crashes. None of that matters.

Only Mommy.

"Mommy, I'm going to make you all better," I tell her as tears roll down my cheeks.

Her lips twitch like she's trying to say something to me but nothing comes out.

"Mommy," I sob, "don't go to sleep."

Please come back, Bones. I need your help!

I'm still trying to help Mommy when I'm snatched away from her. The blood surges from her throat now that I'm not able to hold it closed anymore. I scream and thrash in the arms of whoever has me. It's too soft to be Daddy. This should comfort me but this person is keeping me from helping my Mommy.

"Stop. Kadence, stop."

Grandma's words make me angry. I'm about to hit her—hit my own Grandma—when police and medical people come charging in. I don't know where Daddy is but I'm thankful they're here to take over. They'll sew my mommy up and make her better. Then, they can take my daddy to jail. We'll be happy again.

A policeman says something to Grandma and she releases me. They yammer about I don't know what. I'm scared and sad. Drawing my knees to my chest, I hug them to me and watch them work frantically on Mommy.

I close my eyes.

Maybe this is a dream.

Maybe I can hide...

And when I wake up, it will never have happened.

"Kady Bug?"

The warm voice is right there in my ear but I don't dare open my eyes.

"I'm Officer Joe. Are you okay?" he asks. The man sounds nice. I wish he'd hug me and promise me Mommy will be okay.

"N-No."

"You're safe now. He can't hurt you anymore."

I want to believe the nice man. "Where is Daddy?"

"He's going to jail for a long time."

Peace settles over me knowing we won't have to fear Daddy anymore. Mommy will be safe from his hits. Me and Bones will be safe from the bad stuff he does. And Grandma will be safe too.

"Have you seen Bones?" I ask, still too terrified to open my eyes back up.

He lets out a sad sigh. "Bones is scared too, Kady Bug."

My entire body quivers. Soon Grandma is back at my side hugging me to her. I don't dare open my eyes because I *want this nightmare to be over. I'm ready to wake up and eat Grandma's yummy pancakes. To argue with Bones over what Saturday morning cartoons we're going to watch. I want to wait by my window until I see Yeo riding down the street on his bike.*

Warmth.

This warmth is familiar and I've missed it dearly.

"Where were you?" I demand.

Bones curls up behind me. His body quivers. "I was hiding from him."

"Why? We needed your help!"

Bones starts to cry and it makes me cry too. "Kady, I'm so scared of him."

I swallow down my anger and let sorrow flood through me. I'm so scared of him too. "Don't ever hide from me again," I hiss.

He sniffles. "I promise on all the bags of Cheetos in the world."

A smile graces my lips. At least I know he's serious.

Kady. Kady. Kady.

Black and then screams.

Black and then commotion.

The thick scent of cigarette smoke and cheap beer permeates the air around me. I'm confused and disoriented, still lost in what ended up being a reality and not a nightmare. But it's like my daddy is still here. Like he isn't in jail at all.

"I've got this, Kady."

Bones. Bones. Bones.

His whispered words come at exactly the right time. Bones may have abandoned me that night but he's never done it since. He senses my terror and comes in ready for a fight.

"I love you, Bones."

He doesn't have to say it back because I know.

And on that thought, I delightfully check out.

chapter twenty-four

Bones

I'm trapped between reality and the subspace of Kady's mind. Black and white. Two different windows opening back and forth. I'm straddling the fence on a hunt for that sick fuck. I can smell him. His pungent stink sickens the hell out of me. The child within me has the urge to run far off into the dark shadows to hide from him. Just like when he hurt Kady's mom. When I'd pussied out and left her on her own.

Not this time, asshole.

Unlike the dick who's in prison serving back to back life sentences for the murder of her mother, this alter—as that grandpa dressing fuck calls us—is not the real Norman. The persecuting alter who haunts the dark space in her head is not the man who raped me as a child.

Breathe, Bones.

You've got this.

"Kady!"

Yeo.

On one side of the fence, Yeo is pleading with her. I'm not sure what for exactly and I can't focus on him no matter how fucking sexy he is in his baby blue dress shirt. I can't focus on his parents or Dr. Dweeb who sticks out like a sore thumb in his gay-ass pink shirt.

My focus is on the other side.

Where I know Norman lurks close by. He's practically foaming at the mouth to take over and fuck up her world. In the past, when he's taken over, it's been because I was too much of a pussy to keep him from doing so. I'd relied on Yeo and Officer Joe to help keep him at bay. But now I know, it's all up to me.

I got rid of Kenneth and Pascale.

It's time to take out the rest of the filthy trash.

"Well, if it isn't the pussy boy who likes a good pounding in the ass," Norman growls, his voice sounding like something demonic. "I bet you still think about my cock inside you."

Bile rises in my throat. I clutch my weapon. Desperate times call for desperate measures. Officer Joe has Agatha and the others hidden away safely. Everyone is afraid of Norman.

"I've had bigger. And I've certainly had better," I throw back at him. I'm trying to sound unaffected but my voice holds a slight quiver.

His laughter is evil. It sends a chill rattling through me. "BONES!"

Yeo's roar jolts through me and light blinds me. Fuck! I almost had him. Back to the darkness I go.

I don't have to see Norman in the shadows but I can feel him within inches of me. There's no time. I'll have to make my move now. It's the only chance I'll probably ever get.

"Aunt Suzy!" I holler. "Play my jam!"

Sabotage by Beastie Boys screams all around me. Memories of the past where he took so much from Kady and I swirl around me like a furious fog. Red and hissing and fucking angry as hell. I allow the rage to consume me.

I *will* annihilate him.

"Time to go to hell where you belong," I snarl.

I've still got the steak knife in my grip from dinner. Before the fucker can escape, I stab at him. The blade tears through the muscle in his chest. Ripping and crunching as it inches deep inside of him. I yank it out and plunge it harder into him this time. The music blares around me.

I *will* kill him.

He won't hurt my family anymore.

"You stupid fuck," he bellows. "What have you done?"

And then it's light. He's switched sides but I'm on his heels. The knife feels solid in my grip. Real. Heavy.

I plunge into him again.

Yeo attacks. Why the fuck would he try and stop me from killing Norman? After all the talks we've had about ending him. Why stop me now?

"No!" I roar.

Norman and I are back into the darkness. The knife is light again. Over and over and over again I stab at the abusive motherfucker. Blood splatters the blackness and paints it red. It's like the time I dipped Kady's paintbrush in the red paint at school and flung it at the other kids. It splattered everywhere and made such a pretty mess.

"Oh, Bones," Agatha chides. "What have you done?"

Reminds me of how Ruth had spanked me when the note came home from the teacher. I'd made such a mess. Just like now. I miss Ruth. But that's why we have Agatha now.

"Bones!"

Presley's sobs in the dark confuse me. She never cries. The little girl is always so happy.

"Why is everything so heavy?" I ask.

The music has stopped and everything goes silent. Five faces peer over me. How the fuck did I get on the ground?

They're all crying.

Officer Joe. Aunt Suzy. Agatha. Presley. Whiskers.

"Where's Norman?" My voice is a whisper. Kady loves whispers.

"You did it," Officer Joe says gruffly, his voice hoarse with emotion. "You got rid of him."

And then they're hugging me.

The black is fading.

Dark grey.

Muted grey.

Pale grey.

Off white.

Bright white.

"Bones," Yeo chokes out. "What have you done?"

He's holding me to him. In front of Dr. Dweeb and his parents. I can hear them frantically shouting but my focus is on Yeo.

"You're so fuckin' hot, Kitty Muncher," I whisper.

Tears. Yeo never cries. Yet, tears are spilling down his handsome face.

I raise a shaky hand to swipe them away. My fingers are soaked in blood. Confusion threatens to steal me away from him but I hold onto clarity.

"What happened?"

His jaw clenches and he shakes his head. A loud sob ripples through him as he draws me to him. He presses kisses all over my face. I'm vaguely aware of a pain in my chest. It's as if someone is trying to cut my heart away.

"Yeo…"

He's crying too hard and his cheek is pressed against mine. His mouth whispers a thousand and one lovely words. I like his whispers.

"Bones, I love you." Then he lets out a roar so loud I think the windows may burst. "WHY DID YOU DO THIS?!"

I love Yeo's roars.

My eyes close and I finally manage to piece together what I'd done.

I stabbed Norman.

But I also stabbed *me*.

Which means I stabbed Kady.

Fuck.

When I open my eyes, he's staring down at me. His black eyebrows are pinched together. Those almond shaped eyes are bright red from tears. The stick straight hair on his head is bloody and pointing in every which direction. His full lips are parted. I watch in fascination as the tears streak down his face and slip into his mouth. I bet he tastes salty.

"Why?" he sobs, his dark brown eyes probing mine for answers.

I let out a hiss of pained breath. "Because I had to, Kitty Muncher."

chapter twenty-five

Yeo

I work at a knot forming between my neck and my shoulder. The chiropractor I'd visited last week told me it was stress. That I needed to relax.

With Kady, I can never relax.

With Kady, my life is a constant roar.

With Kady, nothing is easy.

My eyes become fixated on the dried blood beneath my fingernails. I'd half-assed washed my hands upon my mother's insistence a little while ago. Now, I wished I'd have scrubbed all of her blood from me.

Jesus, what had Bones been thinking?

I knew something was wrong when Kady stood up from the dinner table. It all happened so fast. The fear in her eyes. How her body trembled as tears rolled down her cheeks. And then, per usual, Bones swooped in to save her. His determination was intense. But he seemed to flicker like a bright light in the woods. On and off. Off and on.

In between, it was Norman spewing vile things about his daughter that had my mother gagging. I knew they were struggling for power.

Bones got confused.

The lines became blurred.

And the knife Kady had been holding became a weapon of destruction. In his effort to destroy Norman, he destroyed himself.

He stabbed my Kady.

"Still no word?" Evelyn asks my mom.

They're all here. My entire family and Kush. All wearing matching somber faces. All here because they care.

"Not yet," Mom tells her in a hushed voice. "Kadence is still in surgery."

Earlier, Dad tried to assure me that no news was good news. That if they were still working on her, then she had a chance. My heart hangs delicately in the balance, ready to crash to the floor and shatter into a million pieces at any moment. I'm waiting on a few spoken words that will tell me if my life with Kady will continue or if it ends tonight.

"I've never seen anything like it," Kush whispers to my dad. "It was remarkable to see the struggle between the two alters."

I'm not a fan of whispers right now.

"Kush," I grumble. "I love you, man, but now is not the time to analyze shit. Please."

Our eyes meet and he gives me a clipped nod. I bury my face into my palms. While I wait on fate, I let my mind drift to the past.

"It ain't good," Bones tells me over the phone. "I'm telling you, Kitty Muncher, she's lost it."

Ever since I found out Ruth had passed away, I'd been making arrangements to get back to Morgantown. The funeral is tomorrow but I won't get into town until late tonight. I'd hoped to spend time with Kady but from what Bones has told me, she's been scarce.

"What's going on?" I question. "Be straight with me."

He lets out a sigh. From the sound of it, he's tired. Guilt washes over me. I'd left because Kady made me leave. But when I left her, I left him too.

"We got someone new walking these halls…"

I freeze at his words. "Who?"

"You'll see."

"Kady?" *I call out when I step into her house. One quick scan lets me know that Ruth is most definitely gone and that Bones has made a fucking mess of things.* "Bones?"

I step over Cheetos bags littered all over the living room floor and stalk toward the staircase. Footsteps creak upstairs so I take the steps two at a time to find the source. Hers and Bones's rooms are each empty. When I hear humming in Ruth's room, my heart rate picks up. I haven't seen Kady in a year. I've been away at college. She refuses to talk to me. So I talk to Bones about her. It's the closest I can get. At least their voices sound the same. And if I pretend hard enough, I feel like I am talking to Kady.

"Kadydid?"

The humming stops and I rush through the door before she can hide, throwing Bones in her place. When I push through the door, I do a double take. Kady sits in the rocking chair her grandma used to always sit and read in. Ruth's bifocals sit perched on the end of Kady's nose. Her long brown hair has been pulled up into simple bun. Ruth's perfume permeates the air—something old and florally. Kady dons one of Ruth's nightgowns and is wearing her old-as-dirt slippers.

"Uh, Kady," I whisper. Something tells me it's not Kady. And Bones wouldn't be caught dead wearing that shit.

She looks up from her Agatha Christie book and smiles sweetly at me. "Hello, pumpkin. What's your name?"

Disappointment surges through me and emotion grips my throat so that I can't speak. In this moment, I want to scream at the entire world. To yell at God or whoever created this scenario where I could have the girl but she'd be lost inside her own head. That I'd spend my entire life playing hide and seek with her.

I'm exhausted.

Yet, I'm still here.

I'll always be here.

Love doesn't make any goddamned sense.

"You must be the Yeo I've heard so much about. Bones told me you were handsome," she says in a friendly tone. "I'm Agatha."

Her hand reaches for me and I automatically go for it. It's Kady. Somewhere beneath all the old lady garb is my girl. Hiding. Always hiding.

"I've lost my manners," I tell her hoarsely. "My mom would skin me alive. Yeo Anderson. Pleased to meet you."

She takes my hand and it's soft. So fucking soft. I wish I could pull this complicated woman into my arms and draw her out of her own head. That I could whisper her name over and over again until she came crawling from the darkness back into my arms.

"Strong grip for a strong boy," she says with a chuckle. "What's got you so sad, pumpkin?"

My shoulders fall in defeat. I skim the room and my gaze falls on a picture of Bones and Ruth. I know it's Bones in the picture because his face is orange with Cheetos residue. "Bones tell you Ruth passed away?"

My gaze reverts back to hers and she frowns.

"Kady is devastated." Tears well in Agatha's eyes. She waves her book to dry them. "Come sit, kiddo."

Agatha, this new persona dressed in Ruth's clothes but looking so much like my Kady, instantly crawls her way inside my heart. I fall to my knees at her feet and hug her middle. She doesn't hesitate to hug me back. I inhale her. Ruth mixed with Kady. Neither scent is off-putting. Both scents remind me of happier times.

"Where's Kady?" I ask her. "Why won't she see me?"

Agatha strokes my hair and hums a song I remember Ruth used to hum around the house. Finally, she lets out a sad sigh. "I don't know, pumpkin. I really don't know. But I'm glad you're here. You obviously love her. She may be hiding from love," she tells me. "But love will eventually find her."

A painful ache in my chest drags me into the present. I have to quickly blink back the tears. Those years away from Kady had been fucking awful. At first I'd kept up with Bones to keep track of her. But then, every time I turned around, she had a new alter I needed to add to the book. They just kept popping up over the years. Bones, Whiskers, Officer Joe, Agatha, Norman, Kenneth, Presley, Aunt Suzy, and Pascale. I never knew who would answer the phone. It was impossible to predict who would be at the door when I came to visit on my free weekends home.

Bones became more emotionally volatile than he'd ever been. Sometimes he'd tell me to go fuck myself for no reason. Other times, it was like he hung on my every word and practically begged me to sleep with him. I know deep down they were Kady's feelings shining through. Everything got so complicated.

"How you holding up, son?" Dad questions as he sits beside me. He hands me a steaming mug of black coffee.

I shrug my shoulders. "Holding on by a thread to be honest."

He regards me with a grim smile. So many times he'd asked me to stop obsessing over Kady. He'd always sensed that something was wrong with her. The rumor mill in our town was strong and that only fed his opinion of her.

She's crazy.

Her daddy cut her momma's throat right in front of her.

The girl needs to be put in a mental institution.

She talks to herself all the time.

Have you seen how she traipses around half-naked sometimes pretending to be a boy?

It's just so sad when she dresses in her grandma's or her momma's clothes. Someone ought to get that child some counseling.

"She was getting better," he murmurs, mostly to himself.

I sip the coffee and revel in the way it scalds my tongue. I wish it would scald the pain right out of my heart too. "She was."

"What exactly happened at dinner?"

Pinching the bridge of my nose, I let out a huff. "Norman tried to ruin her night. Finally showed his face again. Bones was on a mission to eliminate him like he'd done Pascale and Kenneth. But…"

"Something wasn't right," he states. "She didn't seem all that lucid."

"She wasn't. Kush has been having therapy sessions with her. They'd been identifying her alters. Explaining to them that they were only a part of her and not separate entities. He'd been confident it would help some self-realization occur. For the most part, it had worked. The good ones felt guilty for taking over and the bad ones were confused. She was making such progress. In fact, her alters weren't making many appearances. I'd never had so much Kady time in the entire time I've known her." I scrub my face in frustration. "But I think it made them weak. Bones verbalized this but I don't think I understood the magnitude of what he'd meant. Tonight, Norman reared his ugly head, but Bones wasn't as strong as he'd thought. Kady completely checked out and Bones came to the rescue. I know he didn't mean to stab her, Dad. Bones would never hurt her."

He pats my knee and gives me a firm stare. "He was trying to help. If I had the opportunity to stab her piece of shit father, I would too."

I almost laugh at my dad swearing. Almost. Nothing is laughable right now, though.

"She's going to pull through this," he assures me.

Swallowing, I nod. It's all I've got right now. A huge bucket full of hope.

"When she does, I'd like to make a suggestion." He slips into business mode. "I think you should move in together. I'm not talking about that big, horrible house with a thousand terrible memories. Someplace new. A house in the suburbs or maybe a loft near your practice. Starting fresh could eliminate some of the triggers for her."

The idea isn't a bad one at all. I'm praying to God she does pull through. I'll put a ring on her pretty finger and we can keep trucking on.

Our love is difficult but it's ours and I wouldn't change a thing about it.

"I think you're on to something," I tell him with a half smile. "I'll talk to Kady about it."

I'm sipping on my coffee when a man in scrubs rounds the corner. His face is grim which sends terror rippling through me.

"Are you the family of Kadence Marshall?" he questions. "I'm her surgeon, Dr. Jameson."

I hand Dad my coffee before standing and striding over to him. "I'm her boyfriend, yes. Dr. Anderson."

He rubs the back of his neck before giving me a pointed

stare. "From one doctor to another, I'll be real honest with you. The girl did some damage to herself."

Gritting my teeth, I nod for him to continue.

"She nicked her spleen and punctured her intestines in several places which were our primary concerns." He frowns, and my heart skips several beats. "The bleeding was extensive enough that she required a blood transfusion."

I swallow down my nerves. "Is she okay?"

"We have her stabilized but we're going to keep her in the ICU until we know she's out of the dark for sure."

The hope that had been budding in my chest blooms into something much larger. "This is great news, Dr. Jameson."

He lets out a weary sigh. "That's not all. She also managed to puncture and tear her uterine wall. The hemorrhaging from that organ was the worst." His eyes meet mine and he levels me with his gaze. "It had to be removed."

She'll never bear children.

My heart aches for a family we'll never have.

But right now, none of that matters. Only her.

"Anything else?" My voice is gruff. I sense Dad hovering behind me, soaking up all of the doctor's words.

"They're going to want to run a full psych evaluation on her due to the nature of her self-inflicted injuries."

Kush is suddenly beside me. "I'm her psychiatrist, Dr. Pawan. I'd like to assist in any way I can."

Dr. Jameson looks between us and nods. "I'm grateful to know she has such support."

I glance around at my entire family who have come to stand behind me. Each one wears a sad, worried look. They're here because they love me and have found a place in their heart to care for Kady too.

Together, we're going to get her through this.

chapter twenty-six

Kady

Everything is so quiet.

I feel empty.

Lost inside some never ending dream…not quite a nightmare but nothing pleasant either.

"Kady."

My name, spoken soft and sweet, pulls me from the nothingness. At first, I think it's Bones and I willingly run for it. With my arms wide open and a broad smile on my face, I chase the sound.

But the closer I get, I recognize the voice.

Yeo.

Brilliant colors alight my dark world. A kaleidoscope of love. Red, like the color of Yeo's tongue when he tastes me. Orange, like the color of Bones's Cheetos residue smeared all over his smirking face. Yellow, like the color of Agatha's sponge as she deep cleans the kitchen wearing a pleasant smile that reminds me of my grandma's. Green, like Presley's favorite mint chocolate chip ice cream all over her sticky fingers. Blue, like Officer Joe's concerned eyes hiding behind his aviators. Indigo, like the color of Aunt Suzy's newest obscene lipstick shade painted on her grinning lips. Violet, like the collar Whiskers wears around his furry neck.

A rainbow of love.

And I'm their dark raincloud.

"Kady..."

Kady. Kady. Kady.

Colors fade to black and then I'm blinded by white.

"There you are, beautiful. There you are." His voice is like warm sunshine on my bare legs while sitting in the grass on a summer day. It soaks me through to the bone. Saturates my soul. Heats me to my core. Fills me up with happiness.

Yeo.

I say the word in my head but nothing comes out.

His strong hand envelops mine and he comes into view. My love, so perfect, yet so broken. His normally fierce expression is gone. Blood is smeared on his face. Normally calm, brown pools of chocolate in his eyes flicker with sadness and loss. Red rims the beautiful color as if he's been crying. Black hair is messy and matted on one side with blood. His jaw clenches and unclenches over and over again as if he's physically trying to hold his emotions in.

Free them, I implore him with my gaze.

A tear rolls out of his eye and slips down his cheek. I can't help but smile because he's so damn handsome.

"You made it, Kadydid," he whispers.

God, how I love his whispers.

"Don't try to talk," he tells me. "You still have a tube in your throat."

His thumb strokes the back of my hand. I can't understand why he's so sad. But I can feel it. It radiates from him like heat off a blazing bonfire. I don't like how it burns me from the outside in.

Bones, why is Yeo so sad?

I wait for the familiar smartass remark.

Nothing.

My eyes narrow at Yeo and another tear streams down his cheek. I blink several times. A pounding in my heart begins thudding so loudly, I can hear it. It matches the thundering in my head.

Bones, you promised you wouldn't hide…

I beg him in whispers to come back. And then I roar.

YOU PROMISED ME! YOU PROMISED ME! YOU PROMISED ME, BONES!

The stupid sound of my heart has morphed into a beeping that seems to echo all around me. Yeo rains kisses all over me but panic has set in. I knew it was too quiet. He swipes away my tears but they don't stop. Just a stupid flood of despair pouring from me without an end in sight.

My best friend.

My savior.

The only person in the entire world who knew every dark, dirty detail of my past.

BONES!

A shadow of strength when I was too weak.

A force of hurricane fury when I needed protection.

A scapegoat. A body double. A fill in.

BONES!

The part of my soul that was strong and fearless is gone. With his disappearance, he stole from me. He took what was mine. He robbed me of the part of my heart that was him.

He left me empty.

A battered and torn shell of the real Kady.

Bones.

Yeo's pained face mirrors my own. Somehow he knows. I can't even tell him and he knows. Our friend. The one who put the "terrible" in The Terrible Three is gone. Vanished. Dust in the wind.

"I'm so sorry, Kadydid."

I close my eyes and will this all to be some sort of nightmare. Bones isn't hiding. He's laid up on the couch in my mind, munching on Cheetos, and smoking a blunt. He's bitching about Pascale and Kenneth. He's taunting Presley with tickles, teasing Aunt Suzy with flirtatious grins, and terrorizing Agatha with a slew of curse words she'll no doubt beat him for. He's scheming with Officer Joe and he's petting Whiskers.

And he's loving Yeo.

He's loving *me.*

Bones…

No whispers.

No roars.

Nothing.

Three months later…

"B, A, G, A, B, B, B."

Chase's chubby fingers slowly hit each key but he does it. I beam at him and then clap my hands together.

"Good job. Ready for the next part?" I ask him.

He nods with excitement. Chase suffers from severe social anxiety. I can relate, which is why he feels comfortable taking piano lessons from me. His mother says it's the only time she sees him genuinely happy. And that makes *me* genuinely happy.

It took awhile to heal from my self-inflicted, if you will, injuries. Dr. Jameson allowed Kush to take the lead on my psychological health rather than dumping me off on some unknown doctor at the hospital. As much as I hate discussing the twisted parts of me, Kush somehow allows me to do it in a way that doesn't hurt so bad.

Sure, the ache is ever present.

But he helps soothe the pain when we also talk about the good parts of me. The parts of my past that were happy, whether that be because of my grandma or mom or my alters.

Mostly, the happy parts are because of Yeo.

Kush and I discuss Yeo a lot. It's what keeps me going each time. I don't feel like I'm being ripped apart. Kush helps dissect me in a sterile, clinical way. He teaches me about each part of myself that is confusing or sad. Together, we talk through the memories I repressed. Memories that have done far more internal damage than they ever did externally. He exposes them. He peels back the layers. He points them out under the bright light. I'm forced to face each and every one of them. And I'm finally learning how to do it without shutting down on him.

Not that it matters much anymore.

With the bad alters gone and Bones having been torn from me, the rest have faded. I seek them out. All of them. But they all remain just out of reach. Kush assures me they're doing it because they love me. Sometimes love hurts.

"You ready to go, kiddo?" Chase's mom, Cynthia, calls out.

He slides off the bench seat and runs over to her.

"Don't forget to grab your snack," I tell him. "You did a great job."

Chase gives me a snaggle-toothed smile and takes a small bag of Cheetos from the basket on my desk. She mouths a thank you to me before they head out. I stand from the piano and survey the space around me.

My studio.

I'm still in awe of it.

Once I got well enough to leave the hospital, Yeo had one of the rooms in his building renovated to suit my needs. One wall is nothing but windows that overlook the glistening Monongahela River, and sometimes I find myself curled up on one of the bean bags in front of the glass simply admiring the view. He'd had my piano delivered from my house and had even decorated the space with some of my favorite things. It's painted a fresh, off-white color. I love how inviting and pure and fresh it is.

Now, I teach my piano students here, instead of at my

house that is currently up for sale. He and Kush have even referred some of their patients to me. I'm not certified in music therapy, but it's something I've begun to look into online. Until then, I just continue teaching piano like I normally do. The patients, my students, seem to enjoy themselves. It makes me happy and keeps me busy.

"All done for the day?"

Yeo's deep voice soaks through me like hot steam in a sauna. He's always had such a physical effect on me. I turn and regard my doctor. So handsome today in his black slacks and light grey dress shirt. His tie is loose around his neck and the sleeves of his shirt are rolled up revealing his toned forearms. I bite on my bottom lip before looking up into his chocolate orbs. A smug smile sits on his full lips and I want to kiss it until it becomes mine.

"I missed you," I tell him as I glide over to him. I'm walking on clouds. That's Yeo's effect on me.

He's gentle when he pulls me to him. Ever since the incident, he handles me as if I'm a porcelain figurine, like the ones his mother collects. That he might accidentally hold me in a way that crushes me to dust. I hate that he's afraid.

My body is healed.

It's my heart that's still bleeding.

"Take me home," I tell him.

He looks down at me and kisses me on the nose. "My pleasure."

Hand in hand, we walk down the two flights of stairs and out of his building. Yeo looks both ways before guiding me across the street. A block of newly renovated lofts sits situated between Kush's favorite pizza place and a small bookstore that's been around since the fifties. Home is unit 9B.

Nine alters.

B for Bones.

Yeo shyly admitted that's why he chose that unit. But also, the unit faces his building. It's on the top floor, the biggest of them all, and it's ours. Bad memories don't haunt me here. In fact, it's my second happy place. Together, we've decorated it in a way that tells our story.

He unlocks the door once we're upstairs and I trail in after him. The bright white walls and light grey furniture are modern and inviting. We managed to add color by pulling the colorful parts of our life and showcasing them all over. Presley's artwork is framed and decorates our home. A lamp from my mother's bedroom sits on an end table. All of Grandma's Agatha Christie books line a bookcase by our fireplace. Many family pictures decorate the mantel. Lots of Yeo and I. Some of him and his family. A few of me and my family. Several of my alters. My favorite is the picture in the center.

Bones wears a Beastie Boys black T-shirt and sits on the front porch with a blunt dangling from his lips. His brown eyebrow is lifted up in an amused way. Love lights up his normally troubled eyes. I know Yeo is behind the camera because Bones only ever looked at him that way. As if he was his entire world.

I swipe away a tear when I feel warmth wrap around me from behind.

A different warmth than the past.

Yeo's warmth.

"Patty called earlier and asked if we wanted to have dinner with her and Barclay this weekend. She said she wants you to show her how to make that icebox pie," he murmurs against my hair. His palms hover over my still occasionally sore abdomen. I wish he'd grip my flesh and handle me like old times.

"Okay."

I can feel his smile behind me. I smile too. Twisting in his arms, I ask him the question that's been on my mind a lot lately. "Why won't you have sex with me?"

His cheeks turn slightly pink and his jaw clenches. I can feel him grow hard between us. We both want it. When he's pressed up against me late at night, his erection pokes into me. Yet…he never acts on it. I think he thinks I'm broken.

"You were stabbed multiple times, Kady. And your…" he trails of. His forehead drops to mine and he rests it there with his eyes closed.

I run my palms up the front of his dress shirt and chew on my bottom lip. My uterus had been damaged beyond repair. They took it out. I didn't even have a say in the matter. "My doctor said I'm healthy and healed for sex. I asked him."

His eyes open and he regards me sadly. "I know but…" He swallows and his Adam's apple bobs in his throat. "What if it hurts you?"

I slip my hand between us and grip his cock through his pants causing him to groan with pleasure. "Then we stop. But I want to try, Yeo. Will you try for me? I'm not going to break. I feel good. Stop fearing you're going to hurt me."

He lets out a hiss of breath before his fingers spear into

my messy hair. His mouth crashes to mine. It isn't a soft kiss or gentle in any way. Our teeth clatter together and our tongues duel for ownership.

I let his win…

And my prince, my never-ending force of love, scoops me in his strong, capable arms. He strides with me through the living room and down the hallway. Our kiss never wanes as he enters our room and sets me to my feet. He pulls away long enough to start plucking through the buttons on his shirt. I peel my sweater dress from my body and toss it to the floor. My panties drop next. I'm not wearing a bra. I don't care for them much. I'll blame Bones for that.

As Yeo undresses, my gaze flits to the large framed photos on the wall, all arranged in an artfully done collage. The pictures from the book Yeo made have been blown up and framed. Of course, technically, they're all of me. But I don't see me. I see *them*.

Whiskers. Officer Joe. Agatha. Presley. Aunt Suzy.

And Bones.

The bad alters stay in the book but sometimes I look at them too.

Even Norman.

Kush says I'm brave. That I'm facing my past.

I don't feel brave.

"Are you sure?" Yeo questions, his fingers under my chin. He turns and lifts my head so that we're staring at one another.

"I am."

He grins at me. Such a perfect, beautiful, sexy smile. All mine. This man of mine guides me onto our soft bed. His brows furrow as he regards my scars. Fingertips dance over each one, nothing but a whisper of a feeling.

I like his whispers.

"Yeo..."

Dark eyes penetrate mine. Hunger and need and love so fierce pour from him. I want to drown in him. Death by Yeo. What a way to go...

His soft lips press little kisses all over my mottled flesh. With each intimate touch, my need for him intensifies. Every single nerve ending in my body is alive. They all point to him. They all beg him to touch them. And he does. Yeo is attentive and worships my body. He doesn't rush but instead takes his time.

For what seems like hours he draws pleasure from me.

For what seems like hours he teases me with everything but what I really want.

For what seems like hours he whispers all the ways he loves me.

"YEO!" I roar and buck with need. "I need you!"

His strong, sculpted body climbs over mine. Hot flesh zaps my own and the slick sweat we create sends ripples of excitement rushing through me. I'm kissed with the hunger of a thousand starved men as he teases my now dripping sex with the tip of his perfect cock. Normally, here's the part where my responsible boyfriend would slide on a condom. Not just to protect my body from pregnancy. But also to protect my heart from what-ifs. To protect our future from the horrors of my past.

He pushes into me slowly. Bare and unprotected. In such an aching way that almost has me screaming for him to hurry. But I don't... I dig my fingernails into his firm shoulders and tilt my head back to bare my throat to him. His lips tickle the skin on my neck before he sucks me hard into his mouth. As I cry out, he drives the rest of the way into me. I'm not in pain. But I am I'm dying of pleasure.

"Don't stop," I plead as he begins pumping into me with a cadence that matches that of my heart.

"I'll never stop, Kadydid. Never."

And he doesn't.

Yeo makes love to me with an intensity that won't die with this life. It roars and roars and when we're both long gone from this world, it will ripple with whispers until the end of time.

Pleasure explodes around me and the white room dances with colors.

With a groan, he releases his pleasure inside of me. No barriers anymore. Just Yeo and me. Together, we are finally free.

"I love you at your best and I love you at your worst. I love every single part of you. I always have and always will. I even love the parts I hate about you. How fucking weird is that? And I'll continue to love you in every capacity, no matter how strange that makes me. I'll fill in the missing voids of your heart with parts of mine," he whispers while his cock still twitches inside me. "Together, we'll be whole. I love you, Kadence Marshall. Please marry me."

I love his whispers.

epilogue

Five months later...

Badass Motherfucker

"**W**eddings are gay," I say, a smile playing at my lips. And they kind of are—all flowery and shit. Lame music too.

The little girl with the brown pigtails sticks her tongue out at me. "You big liar. I can tell you like it."

I shrug my shoulders and regard the fancy affair on the banks of the Monongahela River. "Everything's always so...white," I complain. "Where's the black? Where're the Cheetos? Who's hiding the pot? Where's the good music? Who even listens to this shit? Am I right?" I nudge the serious officer beside me.

He only grunts in response. "Drugs are bad."

I snort with laughter.

"White is a symbol of cleanliness, pumpkin. Cleanliness is right there next to godliness," says the old woman wearing her old robe and tattered slippers to the over-the-top frilly gig.

The little girl giggles at her words and I tug at one of her pigtails before regarding the other woman in our group. "What about you, Candy Lips?"

A smile tugs at her bright orange lips and she adjusts her scarf on her head. "I think weddings are beautiful. Especially this one. I thought we'd never get to see it." She swipes at a tear.

Life sometimes calls for exceptions.

Love sometimes demands them.

We'll make an exception this one time.

A cat circling my feet meows, so I pick it up and regard my family as I scratch him behind his ears. All perfect and mine. We don't belong out there with her. That's *her* world. Our home is here. Behind her. Watching her back. Always there to pick her up if she stumbles.

Luckily, she has *him*.

And he'll never let her fall.

That beautiful, strong, resilient loving man will always catch her.

Always.

My heart does a little squeeze in my chest. I don't think that pain will ever go away. The memories stay fresh in my mind and they'll get me through this existence. I'll take them wherever I go.

"Time to go, peeps," I say finally, my gaze lingering on the two better parts of The Terrible Three.

My family moans and groans but they know it's time.

We don't linger anymore.

We let her do her thing.

They do as I say because I'm the motherfucking boss.

"I heard that," the old woman chides.

I grin and snap my fingers. "Candy Lips, my jam."

The little girl hands me a pair of black shades and I trade them for the cat.

Sabotage blares in the background as I run my fingers through my hair. The officer steps in beside me and all three girls flank me from behind. The feisty feline meows.

"Machine gun," I whisper.

When I'm ignored, I roar. "Machine gun!"

The officer shakes his head. "You're such a weirdo." But he hands me my machine gun anyway. Giggles from all my bitches behind me.

"And soap from this one," the old lady gripes.

Oops.

I take the clean smelling bar from her and bite down on it. At this point in my life, I'm getting used to the disgusting taste of the soap. I've been punished on many occasions this way. Sometimes even badass dudes have someone they answer to.

I look over my shoulder for one last glance. *Goodbye, Kady Bug and Kitty Muncher.* Turning from the light, I embrace the darkness. I lead the way for my family and step toward the shadows.

"Let's roll." I toss the bitter soap and gesture for them to follow me. "Time to blow this popsicle stand."

And we do.

Bones is motherfucking out.

The End.

Dear Readers,

Thank you for going on this unusual ride with me. I hope you enjoyed all of the complicated characters that were a part of Kady and Yeo's world. This story sat in my brain for probably an entire year before I even attempted to write it. I knew it would be challenging to write with a ton of research involved. There would be some areas where I'd have to trust you to suspend reality for a bit and just *go with it*. I can't thank you enough for trusting me to give you something entertaining, emotional, thought provoking, and ultimately…an impossible love story.

As you well know now, this story will be ruined by spoilers. I beg of you to keep your honest reviews as vague as possible when it comes to the plot and the big twist. It'll make for a much more enjoyable reading experience for those who come after you.

Thank you,
K Webster

You can learn more about Dissociative Identity Disorder at

www.healthyplace.com/abuse/dissociative-identity-disorder/understanding-dissociative-identity-disorder-alters
and
www.nami.org/Learn-More/Mental-Health-Conditions/Dissociative-Disorders

You can learn more about many different types of alters, including non-human alters like Whiskers at www.traumadissociation.com/alters

You can watch a couple of different videos where people switch between their alters here:

https://www.youtube.com/watch?v=cjemK803l2M#action=share
and
https://www.youtube.com/watch?v=6nfoyoTxpn0#action=share

playlist

Patience – Guns N' Roses
Stand By Me – Otis Redding
Sabotage – Beastie Boys
It's Been Awhile – Staind
Afraid – The Neighbourhood
How Soon Is Now? – The Smiths
Run, Run, Run – Tokio Hotel
Everything In Its Right Place – Radiohead
Black Gives Way To Blue – Alice In Chains
The Red – Chevelle
The Secret Letter – Classical New Age Piano Music
Don't Come Around Here No More – Tom Petty and The Heartbreakers
Where Is My Mind? – Pixies
Closer – Kings of Leon
Hurt – Johnny Cash
Figure It Out – Royal Blood
Mad World (feat. Gary Jules) – Michael Andrews
Behind Blue Eyes – The Who
People Are Strange – The Doors
I Won't Back Down – Tom Petty
Free Fallin' – Tom Petty
Say Hello 2 Heaven – Temple of the Dog
Not an Addict – K's Choice
Mess Is Mine – Vance Joy
Heathens – Twenty One Pilots
Can't Help Falling in Love – Elvis Presley

acknowledgements

Thank you to my husband, Matt. When this story was just a simple concept, you encouraged me to reach in and pull it all out of the depths of my limitless head. Your support means so much. Love you, hunny bunny!

A huge thank you to Lucia Franco for getting me through a huge hump when I was stuck. Just talking it through with you was the little push I needed to power through and finish. If it weren't for you, I'd still be obsessing over said hump. You're an awesome friend!

A big thank you to my author friends who have given me your friendship and your support. You have no idea how much that means to me.

Thank you to all of my blogger friends both big and small that go above and beyond to always share my stuff. You all rock! #AllBlogsMatter

I'm especially thankful for my Krazy for K Webster's Books reader group. You ladies are wonderful with your support and friendship. Each and every single one of you is amazingly supportive and caring.

Thank you Stacey Blake for working through a time crunch and always being so flexible. I love you! I love you! I love you!

A big thanks to my PR gal, Nicole Blanchard. You are fabulous at what you do and keep me on track! And also thank you to The Hype PR gals for sharing the love!

Lastly but certainly not least of all, thank you to all of the wonderful readers out there that are willing to hear my story and enjoy my characters like I do. It means the world to me!

about the author

K Webster is a *USA Today* Bestselling author. Her titles have claimed many bestseller tags in numerous categories, are translated in multiple languages, and have been adapted into audiobooks. She lives in "Tornado Alley" with her husband, two children, and her baby dog named Blue. When she's not writing, she's reading, drinking copious amounts of coffee, and researching aliens.

Keep up with K Webster

Facebook: www.facebook.com/authorkwebster

Blog: authorkwebster.wordpress.com

Twitter: twitter.com/KristiWebster

Email: kristi@authorkwebster.com

Goodreads: www.goodreads.com/user/show/10439773-k-webster

Instagram: instagram.com/kristiwebster

books by k webster

CONTEMPORARY ROMANCE STANDALONES:

Wicked Lies Boys Tell

The Day She Cried

Untimely You

Heath

Sundays are for Hangovers

A Merry Christmas with Judy

Zeke's Eden

Schooled by a Senior

Give Me Yesterday

Sunshine and the Stalker

Bidding for Keeps

B-Sides and Rarities

Conheartists

Cocksure Ace

No Tears with Him

Stroke of Midnight

He Made Me Stay

PARANORMAL ROMANCE STANDALONES:

Apartment 2B

Running Free

Mad Sea

Cold Queen

Bond Deeper Than Blood

Shift of Morals

CINDERELLA TRILOGY:

Stroke of Midnight

Prince Charming

The Glass Slipper

2 LOVERS SERIES:
Text 2 Lovers (Book 1)
Hate 2 Lovers (Book 2)
Thieves 2 Lovers (Book 3)

PRETTY LITTLE DOLLS SERIES:
Pretty Stolen Dolls (Book 1)
Pretty Lost Dolls (Book 2)
Pretty New Doll (Book 3)
Pretty Broken Dolls (Book 4)

THE V GAMES SERIES:
Vlad (Book 1)
Ven (Book 2)
Vas (Book 3)

FOUR FATHERS BOOKS:
Pearson

FOUR SONS BOOKS:
Camden

ELITE SEVEN BOOKS:
Gluttony
Greed

ROYAL BASTARDS MC:
Koyn
Copper

THE VEGAS ACES SERIES:
Rock Country (Book 1)
Rock Heart (Book 2)
Rock Bottom (Book 3)

THE BECOMING HER SERIES:
Becoming Lady Thomas (Book 1)
Becoming Countess Dumont (Book 2)
Becoming Mrs. Benedict (Book 3)

ALPHA & OMEGA DUET:
Alpha & Omega (Book 1)
Omega & Love (Book 2)

ELIZABETH GRAY BOOKS:
Blue Hill Blood
Cognati

Made in the USA
Monee, IL
09 June 2021

70784827R00157